"I'd like to propose a bet..."

Piper had to stand on tiptoe to reach Cal's ear. Since she was pressed against his butt, he wasn't complaining.

"What are we negotiating?" His voice sounded gruff, but some things were definitely beyond his control.

"The Fiesta contract." She didn't retreat. Nope. If anything, she pressed in tighter.

"I'm not stepping away," he warned. If he wanted to bring more veterans out here to Discovery Island to work, he had to have that business.

"I wouldn't ask you to do that...more than once." He felt rather than saw her smile against his throat. Piper had always been honest. It was one of the things he liked about her. Her next words were a whisper meant for him alone. "Loser takes orders from the winner for one night—in bed."

And...whoa.

He hadn't seen that one coming.

"We've always had a certain...chemistry. Aren't you curious?"

Oh, yeah.

"I accept," he growled.

D0752483

Dear Reader,

My husband calls my Discovery Island books my vacation books, and he may have a point. I wrote much of my first Harlequin Blaze book, *Wicked Sexy,* sitting on the bathroom floor of a Tahitian bungalow with a large albino gecko for company. It was the only room with electricity where I wouldn't disturb my sleeping kids—although I'm pretty sure they woke up the first time I spotted Mr. Gecko staring down at me from the thatched roof and nearly launched the laptop at his head.

Pieces of our vacations also made it into *Wicked Nights*. I've always been a fish lover, and not just served up on my plate. I fell in love with snorkeling when a very sexy, itty-bitty-swimsuit-wearing French man in Bora Bora told me to jump into the current and *look* at the fish. I did, and, despite almost drowning, I was hooked. I've tried to share some of the beauty of that underwater world in Piper's dives. While Discovery Island is a figment of my imagination, the kelp forests and damselfish Piper sees are not. And hey, just for you all, I made sure to do my research and swim with sharks before I included them in the book.

There will be a third book—Tag deserves a happily-ever-after—and I'm thinking it's time to vacation again. Where do you think we should go?

Happy reading,

Anne Marsh

Wicked Nights

—

Anne Marsh

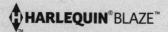
HARLEQUIN® BLAZE™

If you purchased this book without a cover you should be aware that this book is stolen property. It was reported as "unsold and destroyed" to the publisher, and neither the author nor the publisher has received any payment for this "stripped book."

Recycling programs
for this product may
not exist in your area.

ISBN-13: 978-0-373-79819-3

WICKED NIGHTS

Copyright © 2014 by Anne Marsh

All rights reserved. Except for use in any review, the reproduction or utilization of this work in whole or in part in any form by any electronic, mechanical or other means, now known or hereinafter invented, including xerography, photocopying and recording, or in any information storage or retrieval system, is forbidden without the written permission of the publisher, Harlequin Enterprises Limited, 225 Duncan Mill Road, Don Mills, Ontario, Canada M3B 3K9.

This is a work of fiction. Names, characters, places and incidents are either the product of the author's imagination or are used fictitiously, and any resemblance to actual persons, living or dead, business establishments, events or locales is entirely coincidental.

This edition published by arrangement with Harlequin Books S.A.

For questions and comments about the quality of this book, please contact us at CustomerService@Harlequin.com.

® and TM are trademarks of Harlequin Enterprises Limited or its corporate affiliates. Trademarks indicated with ® are registered in the United States Patent and Trademark Office, the Canadian Intellectual Property Office and in other countries.

www.Harlequin.com

Printed in U.S.A.

ABOUT THE AUTHOR

Anne Marsh writes sexy contemporary and paranormal romances because the world can always enjoy one more alpha male. She started writing romance after getting laid off from her job as a technical writer—and quickly decided happily-ever-afters trumped software manuals. She lives in Northern California with her family and six cats.

Books by Anne Marsh

HARLEQUIN BLAZE
805—WICKED SEXY

For Gwen and Kimberley. Books definitely don't write themselves—and you've been with me every step of the way on the road to Harlequin Blaze!

1

PIPER CLARK CUT hard right, the prow of her motorboat slicing through the clear blue water, yards in front of his. He'd have recognized that impish, take-no-prisoners grin anywhere.

Plus, she flipped him the bird as her wake hit his deck, soaking both him and his gear.

Definitely Piper.

Good thing for her he'd grown up in the past twenty years. Cal Brennan's ten-year-old self would have gunned his motor and gotten even, racing her for Discovery Island's marina until he'd swamped her deck every bit as much as she'd swamped his. Tit for tat—those were the rules of engagement they'd always competed by. Still, he picked up speed, hugging her wake—and was just in time to watch as she maneuvered her boat into the last decent slip. Mentally, he readjusted his assessment of his maturity. *Score one for Piper.* He forced his fingers to unclench from the wheel, counted to ten and concentrated on searching out an empty slip. She waved jauntily as he motored past her, close enough to read the name painted on the boat's side. What kind of name was the *Feelin' Free* anyhow?

She'd always named things badly. He distinctly recalled being hit over the head with a stuffed teddy bear named Grand Poo-bah. There had also been a rescue puppy named Mr. Cuddles. Mr. Cuddles had been a mostly deaf white Boxer with a severe drool problem. Mr. Cuddles had moved on to the Happy Hunting grounds some years before, but apparently Piper's lack of naming skills had stuck.

Not that the other four thousand full-time residents on Discovery Island would mind. Twenty-two miles long and eight miles wide, the island's main selling point was its horseshoe-shaped bay with postcard-perfect deep blue water, dotted by boats and two piers. The pier for the cruise ships stretched out into deeper water, but the shorter pier was pure pleasure and clear at the other end of town. The good folks of Discovery Island had named *that* pier Pleasure Pier and the broad strip of creamy, palm-tree-studded sand fronting an old-fashioned boardwalk was Primrose Path. The hotels, shops and restaurants lining the street sported even worse names in Cal's opinion. Good Time, Please Your Eye and Wine, Women and Song. The daily influx of tourists who ferried over from the California coastline to explore the boardwalk loved the names. Or they simply loved diving, fishing, zip-lining or doing any one of the hundreds of activities on offer. Discovery Island was big on keeping busy.

Grabbing his sodden gear bag and his deck shoes, he padded barefoot along the dock, enjoying the heat from the sun-warmed boards soaking into his feet. He and Piper had business, more so than usual. The familiar, soothing noises of the marina washed over him as he fielded greetings from the occasional other boaters and closed in on his target. Discovery Island's marina was a hopping place, but the blue water with its glint of fish and kelp were an invitation to take it easy, as was the familiar bouquet of sea salt, motor oil and Neoprene rubber filling the air.

Lazy waves broke against the docks, slapping fiberglass hulls, and he could just make out the beach boardwalk. On a summer day like today, the place bustled with tourists looking for the quintessential California dream. It was also an ideal day for diving, but he'd stuck to the surface. He hadn't strapped on a tank or even free dived. Not him. He'd had a nice swim, stuck his head under water and promptly panicked.

Just like yesterday.

And every other day since his last dive as a U.S. Navy rescue swimmer. The dive boats he passed, loading and unloading, were an unwelcome reminder of what he'd lost. *Temporarily.* Somehow, he'd get his head on straight, would figure out how to get back in the game and back in the water. He'd never failed before; he wouldn't start now. He had too much riding on his ability to dive.

Turning the corner and spotting Piper's boat was almost a relief. The sighting was definitely a welcome distraction from the panicked voice in his head asking, *What if you don't get back in the game? What if you never dive again?* Hearing voices was never a good sign.

"Piper Clark," he bit out, relieved to have something to *do.* Setting his gear bag down on the dock, he moved to the edge where she'd tied up.

Retreat, the inner voice demanded. *Stand your ground, sailor,* his body urged.

Piper was naked.

Okay, so, she wasn't totally naked, but a man could dream.

Somehow, he'd timed his arrival at her slip for the precise moment she grabbed the zipper running up the back of her wet suit. Undeterred by his presence—because surely she'd heard him snap her name—she pulled, the Neoprene suit parting slow and steady beneath her touch.

Hello.

Each new inch of sun-kissed skin she revealed made certain parts of him spring to life.

If someone had asked him what the over-under was on his seeing Piper naked, he'd have bet heavily against his spotting so much as a sliver of her bare flesh. If he'd expressed an interest, Piper would have shot him down, hard and fast. After all, she didn't like him any more than he liked her. Their shared past was proof of that.

Even as he reminded himself she'd spent most of their early days trying to either torment or kill him, his eyes were busy. Piper's arms were spectacular, strong and toned from hour after hour of pulling herself through the water and then back up into the boat. Diving wasn't for the weak, and she'd had a professional platform-diving career long before the accidental collision five years ago between his boat and her Jet Ski had destroyed her right knee. After she'd rehabbed on the mainland, she'd up and moved full-time to Discovery Island. Island gossip hadn't shared with him the reasons behind the move, but since he'd come back himself, he had to assume she simply loved the place as much as he did. Now she was looking sexier than any stripper, uncovering skin tanned a rich golden brown from time outdoors. The way she'd braided her water-slicked hair in a severe plait only drew his attention to the deceptively vulnerable curve of her neck.

But this was *Piper.*

So dragging his tongue over her skin and tasting all the places where she was still damp from her dive should have been the *last* thing on his mind. He'd read her the riot act about her careless driving and say his piece about tomorrow's business meeting. Then he'd go his way and she'd go hers. After all, he'd been back on the island for almost six months and had managed to avoid all but the briefest of interactions with her. They said hello, goodbye (he suspected she preferred the latter), and nodded tersely at each other from across the street. Life was much quieter that way, because Piper invariably did plenty of yelling when she spent too much time around him.

The wet suit hit her waist.

Neither short nor tall, Piper had medium brown hair, brown eyes and a slim build. Those cut-and-dried facts didn't begin to do the woman in front of him justice, however. They certainly didn't begin to explain why he unexpectedly found her so appealing or why he wanted to wrap an arm around her and take her down to the deck for a kiss. Or seven. He didn't like Piper. He never had. She'd also made it plenty clear he irritated her on a regular basis.

So why was he staring at her like a drowning man?

And...score another point for Piper. Like many divers, she hadn't bothered with a bikini top beneath the three-millimeter wet suit. His kiss quota rocketed up to double digits.

"Piper." His voice sounded hoarse to his own ears. *Focus.* Adrenaline rushed through him, sweat dampening his skin. He forced himself to breathe in, slow and easy. To push his heartbeat down and make the sudden energy pumping through his veins work for him. This wasn't a rapid rappel down to a crash site to search for survivors or a midnight recon of a hostile-infested beach. Nope. This was Discovery Island, a good place with good people. He was home.

Without acknowledging his greeting, she bent over, shoving the heavy suit down her legs, and his throat went dry. *Game over.* Silver earbuds, which explained why she hadn't answered him, flashed as she shimmied, working the suit off. Like always, Piper was lost in her own world, marching to her own beat. Ignorant of his presence, she gave him ample opportunity to admire the longest, sleek-est legs he'd ever seen. Her blue-and-white-striped bikini bottom was all practicality, although the conservative cut still clung to her butt. Her water-darkened braid slid over her shoulder, and he wanted to fist her hair, holding her in place as he ran his hands up those legs and parted her for his kiss. Which made him a first-class bastard, even if he kept those thoughts to himself.

Yeah. But she clearly had more than one advantage on her own side.

He didn't negotiate, he reminded himself. He acted. Decided, he approached the boat, knocking on the side to draw her attention.

She jumped, her head swinging around toward him. "If it isn't my favorite SEAL." She flashed him a grin as she popped the earbuds out, taking in his soaking-wet jeans and damp T-shirt. "Had a mishap?"

She knew precisely what had happened.

He dropped down off the dock, onto her boat. Deliber-ately, he let his feet hit the deck hard, savoring her little flinch. She wasn't as off balance as she'd made him, but it was something. He'd take every advantage he could get because, Christ, she still wasn't wearing a bikini top. In-stead of covering her breasts or grabbing for a towel, she glared at him as if this whole situation was his fault. She was lucky her slip put her out of the line of sight of the other boaters in the marina and he was the only one who could see her. Piper flashed him, and any thoughts he'd had of being a gentleman flew out of his head. He imagined cupping her soft curves in his palms, rubbing his thumbs over the tips. He'd just bet she was a moaner, and—

He jerked his gaze back up to her face. "We've got to talk."

FEET BRACED, LEGS APART, Cal Brennan made himself at home on Piper's deck, nothing but challenge in his gaze as he waited for her to finish checking him out. He was magnificent. And mildly pissed off, which was pretty much the usual state of affairs between her and Cal. Of course, her soaking him when she'd buzzed past him into the marina might explain his foul mood. Faded jeans clung to a pair of powerful legs, and an old cotton T-shirt stretched over broad shoulders. Dog tags flashed as he turned his head to track her. Cal had never needed power suits to scream, "in charge." He moved smoothly, confidently, as he came closer, his bare feet silent on the deck after his initial gunshot-loud landing. Behind him, down the dock, she caught a glimpse of a Harley parked in the street near her dive shop. Cal's black low-rider bike screamed, "race me," followed by, "take me." And, while she'd never considered Cal as dating material, she had to admit he was hot.

Really, really hot.

"We need to talk," he repeated and his patronizing, self-assured tone did a great job dampening the desire blazing a hot path through her belly. His eyes dropped briefly to her breasts again—*darn it*—then returned to her face. Like he was taking inventory and nothing more.

Right. The words coming out of his mouth were perfectly pleasant, but he clearly intended to do all the talking—while she did all the listening. That wasn't how she lived anymore. She wasn't six years old to his ten, any more than she was still a teenage diver bombarded by coaching advice. She was a businesswoman now. A *grown* woman.

Even if being near him made certain parts of her feel like a teenager.

"I'm listening," she said neutrally because there was no point in pissing this man off before she had to. Plus, gazing at him was no hardship. If she was objective (which she usually wasn't when it came to Cal), he looked every bit as sexy as his bike.

Not going there. Swiping her bikini top from her dive bag, she got busy with the ties. While she didn't particularly care about the peep show she'd given him—you got used to stripping down on the dive boat and skin was just skin—she didn't need to introduce the whole male-female thing to this conversation or tempt her hormones any further.

He approached swiftly, inserting himself into her personal space before she could protest. Big, callused fingers brushed the nape of her neck.

"Lift," he ordered. His low, sexy, I'm-in-charge-and-we-both-know-it rasp almost made her forget she'd known Cal for twenty years and liked him for none of that time. She was in so much trouble.

Obediently, she lifted the wet tail of hair while she considered the merits of turning and kneeing him in the balls. Which would be, she decided, a waste. Her body was screaming for satisfaction of a completely different kind, which made no sense at all. She didn't *like* Cal.

"You search me out for a reason? Or did you just stop by for the peep show?" She was proud of herself for calmly getting the words out. She didn't sound like her hormones were rioting at all.

"I'll pick option A." His voice rumbled in her ear as he bent his head and tested the knot he'd made in her bikini top. "I hear you're bidding on the Fiesta Cruise Lines contract."

Fiesta Cruise Lines wanted a local dive shop to run trips for cruise ship clients. Since Fiesta put in one ship a week at Discovery Island, and they'd promised a minimum of twenty divers to start with, the contract was worth a significant chunk of change.

"My interest is no secret."

"Business is booming?"

Her balance sheet wasn't his business. She certainly wasn't going to admit the dive shop she co-owned with her former diving coach wasn't precisely bringing in the bucks. "What do you think?" she asked, turning away from him.

He was silent for a moment. Watching, of course, and probably plotting some terribly efficient course of action. Whatever Cal thought he saw, however, remained a mystery to her.

"I think business has been down on the island overall," he said finally, unfortunately coming to precisely the right conclusion, like he always did. That was one of the most annoying things about Cal. He usually *was* right.

He shifted until he was blocking her path to the dock, unless she crawled over him, which she hadn't done since she was seven. Or maybe nine. Their competitive moments blurred together. What she did know was that she had no plans for full-body contact with him today.

Today.

Whoa. Wrong idea. More clothes would have been good or perhaps a suit of armor. She'd never had the urge to think about Cal naked before. Cal's family owned half the island, and he was the prodigal son who'd come home six months ago after a glorious stint in the military. He'd fought the battles and had the medals and the scars to prove it. She didn't doubt his heroism, but his timing was rotten. She'd come back to Discovery Island two years ago herself to do some starting over and having Cal around now wouldn't make her job any easier. Somehow, she rubbed him the wrong way and he returned the favor. The *last* thing she needed was his brooding self backseat driving or paying any attention at all to her plans for the dive shop.

And he would.

She just knew it.

He'd never, ever cut her any slack, not since the time they'd met when she was six years old and she'd first come to the island with her family for summer vacations in the cheerfully ramshackle, ocean-side cottage that had belonged to her grandmother. The cottage's three bedrooms barely afforded enough room for Piper's parents, her three brothers and herself, but the cozy camping had been part of the appeal. She'd loved those summers. Now the cottage was hers, which was a good thing given how little money she made as a dive instructor. Once she owned Dream Big and Dive outright, however, things would change. She'd be able to expand and to implement some of the ideas she had. All she had to do was win the Fiesta contract so she could convince the bank to loan her the money to buy out her partner.

Cal had driven her six-year-old self crazy. Twenty years later, he'd just gotten better at doing it. Of course, she also knew how to return that favor.

It was strange, though, how much he looked like her definition of a hero. He was a big man, pushing more than six feet. Dark stubble shadowed his jaw like he'd had better things to do than shave and didn't mind living rough. Cal owned the space around him and not merely because he was tall, his wide-legged stance ensuring he easily rode the gentle swell and slap of the marina water against the boat's hull. He was the kind of man who controlled any situation.

She stared at him and he watched her right back. She had the sudden feeling he knew exactly what she was going to do, before she did it. When she stepped away from him, however, his hand slid off her neck and he let her go.

"How are my business plans any of your business?" she replied. Not the politest of questions, but they had a history. He nodded, like she'd just confirmed something he already knew, and she couldn't help but notice he didn't smile. The fine lines around his eyes didn't come from laughter, she realized, but from hours at sea. This man was 100 percent warrior.

And hot enough that she wanted to take him down to the deck herself...

He leaned back against the edge of her dive boat. "Because I'm bidding, too." His dark brown eyes were unnervingly gorgeous. God had definitely not been playing fair the day Cal had been gifted with that feature.

"Tell me you're joking." She kept her voice steady, when she wanted to scream. Unfortunately, she wasn't surprised. Of course Cal would go after the contract she had her eye on.

"Afraid not." He said the two words calmly, as if he hadn't just dropped the mother of all bombshells on her. She needed the contract. *Had* to have it or give up her dream of buying out Del, her partner, because every bank she'd approached so far for the loan had made increased cash flow a condition of borrowing the money.

"Why?" she demanded.

"Because I run a dive center." He made it sound so logical.

"You run a command center," she countered, going on the offensive. "You handle all the search-and-rescue ops for the sector. Why do you want to run dive trips for a cruise ship?"

"Look around you," he said drily. "And then tell me how busy you think I am."

"We've had one tropical storm this summer." Which probably only underscored his point. *One* was singular and nowhere near enough to base a business on. She understood—she just didn't *like* it.

"I want to bring in more former SEALs to lead dive

trips, and it was still a free country, last time I checked. In order to hire more divers, I need to increase our revenue. When I win the Fiesta contract, I do exactly that."

He said it as if the contract was a sure thing.

Maybe it was. He was a veteran and a highly experienced diver. He'd trained U.S. Navy SEALs, the same guys who ensured they *did* still live in the free country Cal had so mockingly mentioned, and there was no way the executives evaluating the proposals wouldn't weigh his military service into the equation. Plus, his plan of hiring former veterans was unspeakably *nice*. Until he'd thrown his name into the ring, she'd seriously had her competition beaten. She narrowed her eyes. Fortunately, she still had a card of her own to play.

"You're not the only one who needs to increase revenue."

"So, business *is* down for you."

It was, and at the worst possible time, too. She needed a beefed-up balance sheet to get her business loan.

She gave him an assessing look. "For you, me and everyone else."

He shrugged. "I heard several other dive shops had submitted a proposal to Fiesta."

"The cruise line has plenty of choices." *Unfortunately.* No, she'd think positive. She was good at what she did and she'd win this one.

The other option wasn't acceptable.

"That contract is mine," she said. She'd visualized nailing each and every dive before she'd climbed the tower in a competition, and she'd do exactly the same here. Cal might be a decorated veteran and combat swimmer, but she was a U.S. national platform-diving champion and a heartbreak story. She didn't like playing the celebrity card, but she'd do whatever it took to win. After her accident, she'd spent two years in the media spotlight, and her name on a dive roster would make people look twice.

He shook his head, shoving off the railing. "Again, it's a free country. You can think what you like."

His tone, however, made it perfectly clear *he,* at least, didn't think she stood a chance.

"You bet."

Dream Big and Dive was her dream and she wasn't letting go. She might not have the cash to purchase Del's interest in the business outright and the banks might have labeled her a poor risk for a business loan, but she'd never gone down without a fight, as Cal knew very well. If she won the Fiesta contract, she won her funding and her shot at making Dream Big and Dive one of the best dive programs for novice divers in California. She'd make it to the final round of bidding, and she'd be in it to win it.

She never lost. Ever.

PIPER CLARK WAS GORGEOUS. Objectively speaking, Cal knew that. What he admired more, however, was the way she met his stare without flinching or dropping her gaze. She was a fighter to the core and Cal's instincts said she wouldn't go down easy. The problem was, she was still his competition for a job he wanted.

Hell.

"You won't win this one," she warned. She stood there, hands parked on her hips as if she owned this competition, and he was certain she believed she did.

"I can." He would, too. His business, Deep Dive, was hands down the best operation in town. Piper, however, clearly believed *she* had the number-one, go-to place on the island. She also radiated an attractive confidence, which would only help her sell it to the Fiesta executives. Her hair was starting to dry now, dark streaks of wet giving

way to lighter brown, and for a woman standing there in a
bikini, she looked remarkably sure. He definitely needed
to date more—or *at all*—because he was fairly certain
he was staring. And that he'd noticed exactly where her
bikini top had left pale white lines on her shoulders. She
had freckles, too, and lots and lots of bare, smooth skin.

Except for her right knee.

She took a step, staggered slightly when the wake from
a passing boat rocked the deck, then righted herself. If he
hadn't been watching her so closely, he'd have missed the
lightning-fast correction. Her knee was the only part of
her that wasn't tanned perfection. The ridges of scar tissue were nothing gruesome—he'd seen far worse during
his military career—and the lines were white. He put a
hand out to steady her and then pulled it back. Yeah. The
look in her eyes said she didn't want help. He'd seen the
same look on the faces of plenty of soldiers. He understood
wanting—no, *needing*—to do things alone. It wasn't as if
he didn't have his own gremlins riding his back, which
was one of many reasons he wanted to bring more veterans
and former teammates on board at Deep Dive. Sometimes,
a guy needed a job and a place to work through his shit.

"You can't stop me," she said, her hands tightening on
her hips.

He shook his head. "Honey, that's where you're wrong."

She smiled at him. "I'm going to win."

"You're so certain?"

"You like to be in charge." Her eyes narrowed accus-
ingly as she went off on one of those Piper tangents he'd
never been able to follow. *Jesus.* Yes, of course he did. The
expression on her face said she did, too. Which was too
bad for her because, not only was he good at it, he held all
the cards here. Instead of responding, he shot her a look.

She shook her head. "No. I don't think so, Cal."

She said his name with the same tone of mocking disgust his SEAL teammates had used when trash talking each other, except her voice held a note of sincerity. He'd seen her breasts. Hell, he'd touched her skin, even if it was only the brush of his fingers against the back of her neck, so it was okay. She could call him anything she wanted, because names didn't bother him. Actions mattered. Not words.

"What are you going to do about it?"

"Win," she said so sweetly his teeth hurt. "That's what I'm going to do, Cal."

Not in his lifetime. "I've got you seriously outgunned here."

"Bet me," she said in the same tone.

He observed her cautiously. Trouble had just shown up on this mission. The playful sparkle in her eyes telegraphed the message loud and clear. Since the only thing she had to be happy about was his leaving the field to her, and he had no intention of doing that, she clearly believed she'd come up with an alternative plan.

"Uh-huh," he drawled, crossing his arms over his chest and leaning in. "What are we betting about?"

"The outcome of the contract negotiations," she clarified, smiling up at him.

"There's only one possible outcome." He dismissed her words with a quick nod. "Deep Dive wins."

"That's what you think." She shrugged casually, clearly baiting her trap.

He'd play.

"It's a fact." Unexpectedly, he didn't want to see her get hurt. If she pulled back now, quietly, she could avoid the agony of defeat and all that. Hell, he almost qualified as a gentleman.

Wicked Nights

"Then, beat me, fair and square." She shot him a fierce grin. "I'll bid. You'll bid."

"I'm not betting you about this."

"Why not?" She leaned forward, bracing her arms on either side of him, on the edge of the dive boat. She wasn't a tall woman and she was careful not to touch him, but somehow she'd turned the tables on him. Again not surprising. Piper had made a career out of shocking him. "Maybe you're just chicken. Put your money where your mouth is, Brennan. Bet me."

"You're not betting money." He wouldn't take her money anyhow. He was almost certain Piper's cash flow left something to be desired. He wanted to beat her, not bankrupt her.

She leaned closer. He tried to pretend her bikini-covered breasts weren't brushing his chest, that her top and his T-shirt were more than enough fabric to keep his imagination from rioting. Piper's breasts were a sweet handful, curvy tops spilling over the edge of her bikini. When she'd been a platform diver, her swimsuit tops had been engineered to compress and create a smooth, sleek line. This top was something else. Feminine. Tempting. And yet— this was *Piper*. He didn't like her, he reminded himself. She didn't like him, even if she loved pushing his buttons. So where had this chemistry come from?

"You're scared." She sounded smug. "We both know I'm winning this one."

And...buttons pushed. "Am not."

Great. He'd regressed to being a three-year-old, except for the part of him that was clearly an adult and wanted to show Piper how much he appreciated her bikini top. Which he wasn't going to do.

A small smile tugged at the corners of her mouth. He knew that smile. He was in so much trouble here. "Are.

Too." She underscored each word with a not-so-subtle poke in his chest.

He captured her fingers in his before she could drill holes into his heart. The words flew out of his mouth before he could think about it.

"Business, Piper. This is strictly business."

"Uh-huh." She gave him a look he couldn't interpret and—he wasn't sure, but did she check him out as she pulled away? Getting a read on Piper was frustrating. "You keep telling yourself that."

2

DISCOVERY ISLAND HAD bars for tourists (all with kitschy names like Devil's Wine and Beer and Skittles) and then there were the places for residents. Diver's Haven was mostly a local scene since the bar was tucked off the main boardwalk. It wasn't precisely a hole-in-the-wall, but the place hadn't exactly earned a prime spot in the local food and wine department, either. It did, however, have cold beer and satellite TV. Tonight, Cal appreciated both. Going head-to-head earlier with Piper had been the icing on a frustrating day of broken equipment, canceled dives and a boat engine leaking enough oil to re-create the *Exxon Valdez.*

The bar propping him up was made from salvaged driftwood, an artistic touch he'd always suspected had been Big Petey, the bar's owner, being cheap rather than fashion-forward, given the booths with cracked vinyl seats. Neon lights in the window advertised brands Big Petey had no intention of stocking and the jukebox worked intermittently, rather like its owner. Big Petey also extended credit to anyone and everyone and had more dishwashers than he did bar glasses because he was incapable of turning down a job seeker. Big Petey was a good man, and he'd never seemed to mind Cal wasn't much of a drinker.

Cal had a one-beer limit. Alcohol wasn't advisable when training, and he wanted his head back in the game. Plus, he'd seen more than one good soldier lose himself inside a bar. So, for the moment, he settled for just sitting at the bar, empty bottle in front of him. The game played on the big screen, and the clack of balls from the pool tables in the back competed with the occasional groan as a batter struck out. Tag and Daeg, fellow former rescue swimmers and current co-owners of Deep Dive, had moved on to the backroom and a game of pool and talking trash. More words flew than balls when those two played, only proving that nothing much had changed since their last tour of duty together. He still thanked his lucky stars every day that he'd been able to convince them to move up here from San Diego and join him rather than reenlisting.

Big Petey looked over at him when a commercial came on. "You ready for another?"

He didn't want to put the man out of business. "If you make it a cola."

Big Petey also didn't stock any name-brand sodas. Local gossip alternately claimed he'd outspent his account with both major distributors or referenced the man's legendary cheapness. Since the stuff Big Petey poured was no better or worse than what Cal had drunk in dozens of overseas ports, and had bubbles, Cal didn't care which version of the story was true.

Big Petey grabbed the dirty glass and stowed it somewhere beneath the bar. "You're making me a rich man, Brennan."

At least he'd merited a clean glass. Maybe. After all, he couldn't see exactly where the new glass Big Petey slapped down on the bar had come from. It was possible his original glass had simply round-tripped. Big Petey aimed the soda gun in the glass's general direction and squeezed.

"Drinks taste a whole heck of a lot better with rum." Big Petey did not have a personal one-beer limit, and Cal's choice of beverage was a constant source of amusement for the other man.

"Big Petey makes an excellent point." The scent of apples and something floral surrounded him as Piper slid onto the empty barstool beside him, resting her bare arms on the counter.

A big grin creased Big Petey's face. "If it isn't our world champion."

Piper made a face. "I didn't compete."

Big Petey grabbed another glass—from the shelf behind him, so definitely clean—and carefully set it down on a cocktail napkin in front of Piper. Piper also merited a bowl of peanuts. If Cal hadn't already known the other man had been nursing a soft spot for Piper, he now had all the proof he needed.

"You'll always be my champion," Big Petey said gruffly. "I'd have been sitting here in the bar, watching you win gold, if you'd gone to the world championships."

Piper smiled and mimed blowing kisses while admiring an imaginary medal. Cal bet it was indeed gold in her imagination. Piper had never settled for being anything but the best. He had no idea how she could handle the constant references to her almost-successes, but she always had a smile when her spot on the team was mentioned, even if she usually changed the topic immediately. She'd had to drop out after the accident because, as superhumanly competitive as Piper was, even she couldn't force her knee to heal fast enough for the world championships.

Sure enough, she pointed to Cal's glass and deflected

Big Petey's interest in her diving dreams. "I'll have what he's having."

Big Petey huffed. "Jack and cola. Coming right up."

Piper snagged a handful of peanuts. "Cal here is predictable. He's downing straight-up soda, and we all know it."

He wasn't that predictable. Was he? He turned on his stool and reached in to steal a handful of peanuts from Piper. And…wow. She hadn't been wearing that dress earlier. In fact, he was certain he'd never seen her sleeveless mint-green number before. Little stripes covered the fabric, making him want to look closer, or maybe it was the woman in the dress. The thing had a neck high enough to pass muster with the most conservative of audiences—apparently he'd seen all he was seeing today of Piper's breasts—but a dearth of fabric south of her butt, stopping a good two inches above her bare knees. She wore a pair of those sandals with laces that wrapped around her ankles and calves and made him think about unwrapping. Piper dressed up was dangerous.

She tugged the peanut bowl out of his reach. "Those are mine."

Her eyes laughed at him, so he snagged a second handful.

"You bet. That's what makes them taste so good."

"You don't change." She sighed dramatically and then raised her glass in the air. "Cheers."

"Right back at you." He clinked his glass against hers. For a few minutes, they nursed their drinks companionably while the home team struck out on the television.

Daeg slid between them, depositing two empty bottles on the bar. "Wow. Now, here's a sight you don't see every day. There's only twelve inches between the two of you, and no one's fighting."

"We don't fight all the time," Piper protested. "And you just took up all the space anyhow."

Daeg eyed the peanuts and she nudged the bowl toward him. "Consider it a public service," he said.

"Hey," Cal protested at the peanut move. "You're discriminating."

Piper flashed him a grin as Big Petey swapped out Daeg's empties. "You bet."

"We get along." Right. Like cats and dogs, oil and water…he could trot out every hackneyed, clichéd comparison and they'd all be accurate. He and Piper fought. Sparred. Lived to one-up each other.

Piper swiveled on her stool, her knee brushing his thigh. He did his best to ignore the small contact.

"Sometimes." Daeg raised his bottle to Piper. "Cheers. But most of the time, the two of you are either fighting or daring each other to do stupid crap. I grew up here, too. I know exactly what the two of you got up to."

Piper shrugged modestly. "What can I say? Cal here is suggestible."

"Someone here is also a sucker for crazy dares," Cal pointed out.

Piper had never met a dare she wouldn't take. She'd done all sorts of crazy things over the years. She'd gone cliff jumping at midnight (which was when he'd discovered his calling as a rescue swimmer). Ridden in a string bikini printed with the American flag down the boardwalk on the back of his Harley (one of his all-time favorite memories). She'd engaged in a very failed attempt at bison tipping, after arguing that the island's bison and cows were more or less interchangeable, and had instead discovered that bison patties stank to high heaven. She'd made him buy her a pair of new sneakers after that one, which he'd thought was fair.

Her grin lit up her face. "You should take more chances."

Over his dead body. "And you're going to kill yourself one of these days."

That was the wrong thing to say. Her hand rubbed the scar on her knee self-consciously. They didn't talk about the Jet Ski accident that had put an end to her diving career. She'd come far too close to dying. Fortunately, he'd completed emergency medical training as part of his rescue-swimmer education. After he'd saved her, he'd staunched the bleeding and thanked God a major artery had been missed. The crystal clear water of Discovery Island had looked like a bad shark attack had occurred that day.

"You up for a game of pool?" She practically jumped off the barstool as she made her getaway.

Daeg looked at him. "Nice going, asshole. Now, go make it up to her."

"By letting her win?"

Cal collected their glasses. He debated grabbing the peanuts, too, but he wasn't a waiter and Piper was already marching across the bar toward the pool tables in the backroom. She clearly expected him to follow, and he felt guilty enough for bringing up bad memories to indulge her.

Daeg shook his head. "No one *lets* Piper do anything. She just does it. She'll win fair and square on her own."

That was true, too. He followed her while he chewed on that one.

The bar's pool table setup was ad hoc at best. Big Petey had gone for the more-is-better approach and shoehorned two pool tables into a space meant for one. The proximity didn't leave a whole lot of room to maneuver.

Piper grabbed a cue stick from the rack on the wall, inspected the tip and leaned her hip against the table. She was good at looking confident. He'd give her that.

"Perfect. You're in," she said when he stepped into the room.

"Piper." Her name came out as a growl.

"Watch," Daeg said to Tag. Apparently, he hadn't been able to resist the promise of a free show. "I'm predicting another crazy bet."

"Twenty bucks," Cal said, knowing she wanted something more than his cash. She probably would negotiate for his shaving his head bald or singing "The Star-Spangled Banner" in a monkey suit when the cruise ship docked, or any other embarrassing trick she could dream up.

"As if." She waved a hand. "I don't play for peanuts. Make it a hundred."

They didn't usually play for cash, but Piper couldn't be making bank at the dive shop. She'd also bought in and owned part of the place, which had probably left her cash poor. Since he had plenty of cash, he was happy to share with her. It would mean losing intentionally, but as long as he made it look good…making sure Piper was fed and happy was worth it. Despite the way they constantly butted heads, he'd never wanted her upset or miserable.

"Ladies first."

She rolled her eyes. "Way to set yourself up for the loss."

He'd played her more times than he could count. Hell. He'd *taught* her to play. She was good, but he was better. He handed their drinks to Daeg and racked the balls.

She tugged on her ear and bent over the table. He'd seen her make the lucky gesture countless times on the diving platform, right before she hurtled through the air and ripped her entry. It must have worked, because she broke straight on, the balls scattering.

When the five ball rolled into the pocket, she straightened up. "Stripes. My favorite. It must be my lucky night."

PIPER HAD NO idea why she'd gotten dressed up just to swing by Big Petey's place. She'd been bored and lonely, though, going more than a little stir-crazy out at her place alone, so she'd hopped into her truck. Possibly, she'd headed here because she was almost certain to find Cal nursing a soda if he was at loose ends. Needling him was pure fun, plus the man seriously begged for a shaking up. Mr. Safety lived and played by the rules.

Growing up, their crazy bets had been a regular summer occurrence. She'd come out to Discovery Island and spend two months indulging in soft-serve ice cream, motorboat rides—and daring Cal. Even then, before he'd become a U.S. Navy rescue swimmer and moved on to rescuing the more deserving than she, he'd wanted to save her from herself.

She'd always been the bigger daredevil of the two of them. He'd rise to the occasion, but invariably remained so serious during the execution of their bets. He was a good sport when he lost, too, although he never lost by nearly as much as she wanted him to. Cal excelled at strategic thinking and, once he was in, he was all in.

She looked over at him, taking his measure. He didn't look worried about their current bet. "You remember the last time we played pool?"

"Four years ago?" He sounded certain.

"The game that ended with you skinny-dipping in the mayor's pool?"

He hadn't expected to lose that particular game of pool, but he'd walked the four blocks to the mayor's house, with her tagging along. Then he'd hopped the fence, lent her a hand as she scrambled over the top, awkwardly because her knee had been a hot mess, and proceeded to nonchalantly strip off. Good times. She'd give Cal credit. He always kept his word.

"Some things are hard to forget," he agreed.

She wondered if now was the time to admit she'd snapped not one but six pictures of his amazing butt as he'd jumped into the pool. She'd hung on to those pictures, too, although she planned on claiming they were blackmail material.

Like them all, he was a little older now, but she'd bet he still looked spectacular naked. When she'd walked into the bar, he'd been staring at his empty soda glass, lost in thought. The scruff on his jaw and the faded pair of blue jeans and polo shirt weren't military issue, but there was no mistaking him for anything but a soldier. He'd also looked alone somehow, even in the middle of the bar's cheerful chaos, and that wasn't right. Sliding onto the stool beside him had seemed natural.

Imagine that.

While she and Cal had never been enemies, they'd never been close friends, either. Between competing to one-up each other and his annoying insistence he knew best, they'd been at odds more often than not, and the days of simply hanging out together had ended with her family vacations. He'd joined the U.S. Navy; she'd gone to college and been headed for a professional diving career. All of which meant they'd met up infrequently in the past few years. And yet…it certainly hadn't escaped *her* attention that they invariably rubbed each other the wrong way when they shared air space.

Grasping the base of the cue with her right hand, she rested the stick on the edge of the table. "You might want to back up. Bodily injury isn't on tonight's agenda."

"Thank God," Daeg muttered behind them and took a drink of what she was fairly certain was her soda.

Spreading her legs slightly, she leaned in and lined up the tip against the cue ball. "Three ball."

Take that. Her shot produced a smooth, fast line to the ball, and it dropped into the pocket with a satisfying thud.

"Seven ball." This time, it took a softer touch to send the ball into the pocket.

Daeg whooped. "She's taking you to the cleaners."

Then, darn it, the four ball ricocheted off the table's side, and she knocked one of Cal's balls into the pocket.

"My turn," he announced, satisfaction filling his voice.

CAL BIT BACK a grin. That was his Piper. She'd gone all out, and her all-in strategy had backfired. Spectacularly. If he sank his seven balls, the game was his. So much for losing intentionally.

He looked over at her. "What do you think I should buy with my hundred bucks?"

He wouldn't actually take her money, but teasing her was too much fun to resist. She belted out a curse and stepped away.

"Didn't I hear you were trying to stop cursing?" His mother had pointedly mentioned Piper's endeavor, apparently under the mistaken belief Cal might want to try the same himself.

He picked out a cue stick from the rack while he waited for her answer.

Her yes, when it came, was grudging. "I'll put a quarter in the swear jar later."

He didn't know where Piper had learned to curse, but she could definitely outswear many of the SEALs he'd served with. Plus, not only was she creative, but she was loud. Her jar probably held enough quarters to fund an entire new wing for the library she'd apparently announced was the jar's beneficiary. Over the course of the next ten minutes, he proceeded to sink his seven balls, one after the other, and Piper's obligations to the swear jar grew more substantial.

Tag whistled. "I shouldn't have bet against you."

She stepped up behind him as he eyed his final shot. It was game over as soon as he sank the eight ball. "I'd like to propose a side bet unrelated to this game," she said.

This game. Not *a* game.

His critical-thinking skills suddenly became nonexistent, which was probably part of Piper's master plan. She had to stand on tiptoe to reach his ear. God knew what it looked like to the other guys in the bar. Since her front was pressed against his butt, he wasn't complaining.

"What are we negotiating?" His voice sounded gruff, but some things were definitely beyond his control.

"The Fiesta contract." She didn't retreat. Nope. If anything, she pressed in tighter.

"I'm not stepping away," he warned. If he wanted to bring more veterans out here to Discovery Island to work, he had to have the additional business. No pool game got in the way of that.

"I wouldn't ask you to bow out…more than once." He felt rather than saw her smile against his throat. Piper had always been honest. It was one of the things he liked about her. Her next words were a whisper meant for him alone. "Loser takes orders from the winner for one night—in bed."

Whoa. He hadn't seen this bet coming.

"You're crazy." Of course, he'd known that for years. Piper had never met a chance she didn't want to take. Twice.

"If you're so sure you're going to win, you've got nothing to worry about."

He looked down at her arms, caging him in place, and wondered if she'd thought her bet all the way through.

"There are other ways to take a man to bed, Piper, if you're desperate."

The bar's noise gave them just enough privacy that the others couldn't hear their low-voiced exchange, but this still wasn't a conversation he wanted to have in public.

She gave a little laugh. "I'm not desperate, Cal."

He eyed his cue stick and wondered what his next step should be. "Then, maybe you could explain it to me."

"We've always had a certain…chemistry. Aren't you curious?"

Oh, yeah, his inner bad boy growled.

"I'm going to take my shot," he warned, all thoughts of deliberately throwing their match vanishing. "I'm winning. You don't want to give me that kind of opening."

"Go right ahead," she said, and he had no idea what she was inviting him to do. And then…she blew on his ear. Right as he shot.

He scratched, the eight ball rolling into the pocket. Well…hell.

She stepped away. "Too bad, Cal. You lose."

Scratching the eight ball was an automatic loss. Piper was clever. And at least now he wouldn't worry about her grocery money for the week.

"You going to pay up?" She parked her butt on the edge of the table and smiled at him. "Because I think we're done here."

He pulled out his wallet from his back pocket and handed over a hundred. Had she even been serious about their new bet?

"You shouldn't walk around with this much cash in your wallet. Someone might take advantage of you."

She hopped down and started for the door, and the sassy twitch to her hips was the last straw. He opened his mouth.

"Drinks are on me tonight," she called back, pouring oil on his fire.

"Piper." Her name shot out before he could stop himself.

"Yeah?"

"I accept," he growled.

3

PIPER BREEZED INTO the conference room with precisely one minute to spare. Cal wondered briefly if she'd sat outside, timing her arrival for maximum impact. Probably. Piper had always loved pushing boundaries, pushing buttons.

Particularly *his* buttons.

He, on the other hand, had shown up early for the meeting with the Fiesta Cruise Lines team, tested his equipment and made small talk with the visiting executives, getting a feel for the terrain. His audience today consisted of two males, one female, all somewhere between forty and fifty-five. Sal Britten, Ben Lloyd and Margie Kemp were recreational divers who had logged some fairly adventurous dives. He didn't anticipate any difficulty selling them on his planned program.

Piper dropped a mammoth white tote bag onto the chair beside him. "Did you miss me? Getting anxious?"

He shot her a look.

She grinned back. "You were. That's positively sweet. I'd almost think you were looking *forward* to losing. To me. Maybe you've been thinking about it since our game earlier this week?"

Her eyes twinkled as she needled him. She wore a white

dress that stopped several inches above her bare knees. The perfectly modest V-neck showed no cleavage but drew his eye anyhow, as did the narrow brown leather belt wrapped around her waist beneath the fitted blue-and-white-striped blazer. She looked fresh and energetic. The cruise ship woman eyed her outfit and he could practically feel the two guys melting. Piper had that winning effect on people.

"I'm not falling for your game," he warned softly.

"And I'm not playing."

She turned away to introduce herself to the Fiesta executives, rings flashing on her fingers as she worked the room. He eyed her ring finger and discovered it was bare. Of course, he couldn't imagine who would take her on for keeps, but there were plenty of crazy men out there. Or men who'd abandon caution when they got a good look at those high-heeled shoes of hers, which made him think of bondage clubs. Not, of course, that he'd ever been to one, but he had internet, and the tan straps crisscrossing her feet were suggestive.

She finished her meet and greet and turned back to him. Sal Britten paused in the middle of a long-winded story about his most recent shark-cage dive off the coast of Australia (Cal would have killed for a look at the man's logbook, because he had his doubts about the man's dive creds) and looked between them. "Do you two know each other?"

"You *bet*," he said, deliberately needling her.

Piper's eyes narrowed, then she winked at him. "Cal here was hoping I'd be a no-show."

If Piper didn't get her butt in gear soon, they'd run late, so he ignored the wink and headed for the back of the room. "This meeting starts now."

She grinned at him, keeping pace with him. "Ready to lose, big boy?"

She made everything into a competition, a game. He was tired of it, frankly, but she wouldn't let it go. If she wanted to *compete,* he'd compete. He was a SEAL. He didn't ring out. He didn't quit. *Except when it came to diving,* the unwelcome voice in his head pointed out.

The cruise ship guy looked over at them. "We're ready to get started when you are. Who's up first?"

Time for the opening salvo. "Ladies first. I insist."

PIPER KEPT HER professional smile painted on her face, but her rescue swimmer wasn't playing fair. Cal waved her to the front of the room, inviting her to lead off the pitches with a lethally charming, "Ladies first," when they both knew going first was the weaker position. Their judges would hold back on scoring to leave room for the last diver.

He grinned and settled back in his seat, arms folded over his chest. If he looked good in nothing more than a pair of jeans and a faded cotton T-shirt, he cleaned up even better. He wore an open-necked shirt—she'd never seen Cal bother with a tie for anything other than funerals and weddings—and a dark suit jacket, which didn't disguise the breadth and power of his shoulders. He had the build of a swimmer, his body advertising that it was trained to pull him through the water at a killer pace. She'd seen him swim, and it was a thing of beauty. She'd give him that much credit.

He was also big and bad, irritatingly calm as he sank back onto his seat, leaning slightly away from her, his legs stretched out in front of him, his arms crossed over his chest. The conference-room table hid his feet, and she fought the urge to peek and see if he was wearing steel-toed work boots. It was hard to imagine him in dress shoes, but he radiated control and competence.

He raised an eyebrow. Right. Her pitch. She hadn't prepared slides or a formal talk, but she knew her message. She'd also loaded up her laptop with images she'd shot at the diving sites she was promoting, because a picture was definitely worth a thousand words. All she had to do was get Sal, Ben and Margie to imagine themselves in those waters, and she'd have them. She quickly tugged on her ear, hoping the lucky gesture would bring her the same good fortune she'd had every time she'd climbed the dive tower and competed.

"You've got a cruise ship full of passengers, most of whom have never dived before. The number of newbies seriously outweighs the number of certified divers. I'd like to go after that segment, grow your tour numbers. Why *wouldn't* those passengers want to dive?"

She'd fallen in love with recreational diving during her own summer trips to Discovery Island. As soon as she'd turned twelve, she'd been fitted up with gear and taught to dive. Her first excursions had been off Discovery Island pier, fifteen-footers, where she could have dived to the bottom without the gas, but the tank meant she could stay under for thirty minutes. She'd loved it and she'd been hooked. Sharing her passion through her dive program just seemed...natural.

Cal sprawled in the back of the room, all hot-eyed, hard-bodied charm as she started walking the executives through a cost comparison of land-based tours with diving excursions. There was more money to be made on booking diving than most of the other shore excursions, and pretty soon her audience of three was nodding along. Except for Cal, of course. His expression said he wasn't convinced.

"If the passengers have never dived before, are you proposing resort dives?"

"Good question." She smiled at the woman and launched into the next part of her talk, walking the room through the shallow, baptismal dives she'd planned for the harbor as she displayed different images on the screen. At thirteen to fifteen feet, anyone in reasonable physical health could give diving a try. Pointing out the window at the gorgeous, light turquoise water, she asked, "Who wouldn't want to get in there and see what's happening beneath the surface?"

Cal raised a brow. She knew that look of mocking disbelief. It was, she decided, too bad for him she had every intention of winning this contract and wiping the smug look off his face.

PIPER HAD THE room in the palm of her hand, which further irritated Cal. Letting her go first had seemed like a smart tactical move, but now he was second-guessing himself. She'd been every bit as unprepared as he'd expected, talking off the cuff without a formal set of slides—and she'd captivated the room with her charm and casual photos. The Fiesta executives leaned forward in their seats, hanging on her every word as she walked them through a novice dive. Her sassy suit probably didn't hurt, either, because looking at her while she talked was no hardship.

She strolled past him as she returned to her seat, mouthing, "Gotcha," and then shifted her monstrosity of a bag to *his* seat when he stood up.

If she thought he was going down without a fight, she was even crazier than he remembered. The Piper of his childhood had relished a good fight. Even as a girl (or maybe because she was a girl with three older brothers), she'd always done her best to outrun, outjump and generally outdo anyone who crossed her path. She would have made an excellent SEAL, if Uncle Sam allowed women on the team. So he bumped her shoulder casually with his hip, leaned down and whispered *sotto voce* in the most condescending tone he could dredge up, "Good job, Piper."

He wasn't going to make this easy for her at all.

Firing up his PowerPoint presentation, he started stepping his audience through the slides. He'd planned a series of challenging adventure dives, along with a mission theme and faux combat training for college-aged divers and older. "All of our dive masters are former Navy SEALs. We can train divers to get to the next level."

The female executive looked intrigued. "So you're proposing extreme diving."

"We'll coach you to dive like a U.S. Navy SEAL." He gave her a winning smile. "I think you'd enjoy it."

Piper stirred in the back of the room. Clearly, she'd concluded that the business portion of today's agenda was done and the executives wouldn't see her unless they turned around. She put her feet up on the chair (*his* chair), stretching her legs out in front of her, and he wondered briefly if her knee hurt. Then he stared at her long legs and those shoes…. Those shoes should be illegal. She stretched and her dress fell up her thigh. He swallowed. Paused. *Danger.*

Quickly, he advanced to the next slide, explaining the SEAL-style obstacle course Deep Dive was building. Or, rather, Tag and Daeg were building, because Cal's head still refused to get with the program. He was useless in the water, which made winning this contract that much more important. At least he could contribute here.

Piper shifted and the final shreds of his focus flew out the window. The room was warm, and in a nod to the heat, she slid off the jacket. The move pulled the material of her dress tight across her breasts, making it clear that her lingerie of choice for today's business meeting had been a pink-and-black bra, despite, or perhaps because of, her white dress. Typical Piper. She loved bold statements.

And he was staring.

Focus, sailor.

He wouldn't be distracted by happy-go-lucky, viciously competitive Piper Clark again. Although…his eyes narrowed even as he kept a pleasant smile plastered on his face. What were the odds she was doing this on purpose? She lifted her arms, twisting her hair up into a loose knot. Ran her fingers down her throat. His imagination rioted, and his body behaved as if it hadn't gotten the memo he didn't *like* Piper.

Definitely on purpose.

She fiddled with the buckles on her shoes, fingers stroking over her ankles, leg drawn up. The shadow of her dress on her thigh prevented him from seeing too high, but if she moved another inch, he'd have a clear shot of paradise.

He was going to kill her.

Ten minutes later, they wrapped up the meeting and headed for the door, the cruise ship executives promising a call in the next couple days. Cal had no idea what he'd said at the end, but it must have sounded okay because nobody was staring at him with pity in their eyes or a smirk on their lips.

"Nice job in there," Piper said, falling into step beside him, but her smile didn't reach her eyes. Was she being polite, or did she feel threatened?

"You cheated." He strode toward the elevator.

"Excuse me?" He could hear the laughter in her voice. She knew precisely what he meant.

"The—" he waved a hand "—shoe thing you did in there wasn't nice. Or fair."

"From where I was standing, you were the competition."

"Sitting," he muttered, before he could stop himself. "And what you did was definitely cheating."

"Did I distract you?"

"Piper." He leaned over her to reach the elevator buttons first. "You showed me the goods. In a *business* meeting."

"I'll take that as a yes. Mission accomplished. I'm going to win our bet, Cal. Maybe you should prepare yourself."

She brushed past him into the elevator, and there was no way she mistook his attraction to her. He, on the other hand, decided to take the stairs. Followed by a ten-mile run.

4

PIPER HAD DISCOVERED her love of jumping when she was two. That was the story her mother told, at any rate. Toddler Piper had climbed up onto the back of the couch and then jumped off, both chubby fists raised in the air over her head. After achieving a remarkable amount of air for someone who'd weighed a mere twenty pounds, she'd crash-landed on the family dog, who'd proved to be both a good sport and an ally, letting her repeat her jump move twice more before her mother had been alerted by the noise and intervened.

When she was five, she'd discovered the springboard at the community pool. Then, at ten, she'd joined the local swim team. Racing was fun, but diving was better. When she'd dived, she'd flown. Performing gymnastics midair was an adrenaline rush better than any jump, and she'd ripped through the water leaving almost no trace of her entry. She'd won every meet and moved on to college and the NCAA championships. A berth on the national team headed to the world championships? No problem. She'd earned that, too. She'd been the golden child, the star diver—right up until she wasn't. It had turned out the one thing Piper's diving career hadn't prepared her for was losing.

The Accident—and she always thought of the day in capital letters—had been just that. An accident. And it hadn't happened at the pool, either. She hadn't made a misstep on her vault or misjudged her somersault or twist. She simply hadn't *known* Lance Peterson had started drinking at eight o'clock in the morning and stopped approximately twenty minutes before he'd invited her to take a spin on a Jet Ski with him. He'd seemed fine, but no, in the absence of an open container in his hand, she hadn't insisted on a Breathalyzer or quizzed him on his drinking. Hindsight, however, was everything.

Being naively oblivious, she'd hopped on the Jet Ski when Lance had invited her to ride, because it had been that kind of afternoon: a group of casual friends hanging on the beach and enjoying ice cream and the sunshine. In the middle of the harbor, she'd realized Lance was impaired when her close proximity to him had made misinterpreting the alcoholic fumes wafting from him impossible. Of *course* she'd promptly snapped, "Go back," in his ear, digging her arms tighter around his waist. Driving drunk was horrifically stupid, and she'd already been measuring the distance to shore. The swim hadn't looked too bad, although even she had preferred not to take a chance with all the boat traffic zipping through the harbor. Unfortunately, Lance had made an easy dismount impossible, cutting in and out, whooping as he'd driven the Jet Ski left and then right. She'd have to pick her moment or convince him to head back.

"Lance—" She'd gotten his name out, Cal's motorboat had come around the breakwater and Lance had cut it too close. So close that she'd seen Cal's face, the look of fierce, calm concentration as he'd thrown the wheel right, ramming the boat into the breakwater as he'd tried to avoid the smashup. They'd hit anyhow. The Jet Ski had smashed into her leg as they'd flipped, and the whole world had narrowed to the pain radiating through her knee as she'd sunk down, eyes open. She didn't have too many memories after the initial impact, which doctors had assured her was her body's way of coping with the trauma. She did, however, remember Cal ripping through the surface of the water, swimming hard and fast to get to her.

Now, for the first time since the accident, she was standing on her own two feet. She had a loving, protective, competitive family back on the mainland. Her family had suggested medical school and then law school, before all but begging her to join the family business. She didn't want that.

Her family was a ranch family. Her great-grandfather had started a small almond farm in midstate California, and the rest of the family had stuck close. Moneywise, there was more than enough in the good years—but they'd never made get-rich money. Other than summers on Discovery Island, her childhood had been full of tractors, ATVs, horses and trails. She'd spent more time outdoors than in, excelling in 4H competitions, winning blue ribbons and awards. Sure, she could have gone home, and they'd have made room for her in the family business, but…she wanted to create one of her own.

She didn't want anything handed to her. Her three brothers had all happily settled down to ranch, competing amiably to see who could claim the most rodeo buckles, grow the biggest crop or innovate the most. Diving had made sense to them when she'd been diving for a berth on a national team, but owning a dive shop on a vacation island wasn't aspirational enough for them. None of them had accepted that her new dream included four walls, a some-times temperamental dive boat and racks of tanks.

Dream Big and Dive's name came from the heart. Piper had learned firsthand that you had to let go of some dreams, but this time she was holding on. She wasn't let-ting Cal Brennan beat her, not when her shot at owning the dive shop was on the line. Her soon-to-be place had a prime location, right off the boardwalk fronting the water, with plenty of foot traffic and easy access to both the ma-rina and the beach where she loaded the dive boats.

Standing there in the front of the shop, she could just read the chalkboard outside, announcing the week's dive sites and inviting newbies to come on in and sign up for a baptismal dive.

Her cell phone rang, blaring the *Jaws* theme song. Right now, the ringtone was all too appropriate. Her partner, Del Rogers, was the shark circling in her waters. Her former coach had franchised a string of dive shops in California and Hawaii, including Dream Big and Dive. Del had won dozens of gold medals and multiple U.S. championships, and photos of him caught in midair as he dived off the platform covered the wall in his San Diego office. He was a force to be reckoned with, and unfortunately for her, he was entertaining an offer on the shop. An all-cash, super-attractive and almost-impossible-to-beat offer. The offer worried her, but she'd made a career of winning, and she'd overcome the odds this time, too.

"Piper," he barked in the same voice that had demanded more of her fifteen-year-old self. More sit-ups, more push-ups, more air or more rotations. She'd always given it to him, and he'd coached her to be the very best.

"Good to hear your voice." *Not.*

No chitchat. Del went straight to business. "Have you made a decision on the Discovery Island site?"

"I still want to buy out your interest," she said, playing for time. Her desires weren't the problem. Finding the cash was.

"Good." There was a brief pause—she'd spent more time hanging in the air over the pool—followed by, "When?"

"I've got a meeting with the bank in two weeks." Of course, talk was cheap. All she'd had to do to *get* the meeting was pick up the phone and dial. Unless she changed her cash flow, however, the outcome would be the same as the past two meetings. The banking professional would listen—professionally—and then recommend her application be denied.

"I'm going to take that offer for my share." And…with nine words, Del benched her. She fought the urge to fling the phone because she couldn't afford to replace her phone and she definitely couldn't afford to buy the dive shop. "Money talks and cash sounds mighty good to me."

"Del—"

He talked over her. "You've had a month to meet my asking price. I need to unload the place. It's not cash flowing, and I'm overextended as it is."

"I'm closing the Fiesta contract. Give me two weeks." She was convinced she could turn the shop around and bring in enough business to make the place viable. Del, however, remained unconvinced.

"This is business."

Her business.

Del had never accepted excuses. He'd always said, "Show me." She scrambled for something to sway him. "Have I ever not won? You know how I perform in crunch situations."

The brief pause on the other end lasted a year. Possibly

three. Piper wasn't entirely sure, but time slowed down in a very *Matrix*-like way.

Del exhaled roughly. "Two weeks. I won't accept any offers for two weeks. If your offer isn't in my hands, it's game over."

"Got it."

She had her time. Now all she had to do was deliver. She was used to crunch situations and performing under pressure. *Just pretend you're climbing the dive tower, mere points out of the lead. One perfect dive.* That was all it would take.

5

PIPER RODE HER Harley down to the Pleasure Pier. A little sugar, a little fun. That was what she needed after her unwelcome call with Del had torpedoed her afternoon, and the Pleasure Pier was perfect.

Built more than a hundred years ago by one of Cal's enterprising island ancestors, a man who'd decided to combine beer sales with fish sales (pure genius, in Piper's opinion), the pier stretched out into the bay, living up to its name. The piles were painted the green of Doublemint gum and winked with white lights. The place stayed true to its roots, selling fishing licenses and fresh fish. The occasional angler parked on the edge, trying his luck in the water below before hauling the catch over to the weighing stations and a dusty wall of old photos of oversized, prize-winning marlin and swordfish, and successful fishermen. For the less fish-inclined, the pier sold saltwater taffy, ice cream and churros. An old-fashioned lemon-yellow swing ride lit up the far end by the beer kiosk.

A beer and candy sounded perfect, followed by a half-dozen, gut-churning rides on the swings. She wanted to fly through the air, leaving the day's problems behind her. Ten minutes later, she traded in five bucks she should have been saving and acquired a fistful of paper tickets and a bonus bag of taffy. She'd passed on the beer, after all— she had the Harley, and some chances she wouldn't take.

The swings slowed, riders stumbling away, laughing. Kids shrieked while their parents snapped photos, creating a scene that was loudly happy and all chaos. *Perfect*.

"Hey, Lenny." She greeted the ticket taker, offering him the bag of taffy. Lenny had worked on the pier for as long as she could remember. Like the ride itself, he looked a little older each year.

"Haven't seen you in a while." Lenny poked through the bag, looking for the red-and-white taffy, like he always did. "Got your favorite swing all ready for you."

"Perfect." She laughed. Her feet flew to the bright red double swing she always rode. Deliciously garish, with over-the-top gold trim covering every edge, and faux rubies hot-glued to the sides, her swing winked at her just as enticingly now as it had twenty years ago. It also had the most lift of all the swings on the ride, or so she and her brothers had concluded after a summer of experimenting. She'd ridden it ever since.

She settled in, waiting for the ride to fill up. The sky was dark now, with plenty of stars peeking through the clouds. She'd always meant to buy one of those charts and learn their names. She tracked one glowing blob and debated if the slowly moving light was a comet or a shooting star. Her knowledge of astronomy was sadly lacking. She'd seen a shooting star once, a bright flare and a quick descent. The flash of red was her first clue that celestial milestones weren't in her future tonight. Her "star" was a plane. Nope. She'd better not count on a career as an astronomer.

And...darn it. Despite her careful planning to *not* think about Cal or the bet she had impulsively proposed to him,

Mr. Tall, Dark and Glum himself stood there on the pier, dogging her from the shadows. The Pleasure Pier wasn't his kind of scene. She had a hard time imagining him fisting a bag of taffy and riding the swings until he was deliciously seasick. Cal was too responsible, too…something else. On the other hand, if she accidentally fell over the pier because she was too dizzy, he'd be the first one in to save her.

He watched from a distance, giving the impression there was an invisible space bubble or do-not-cross police tape surrounding him. The pier's usual evening crowd flowed around him obediently. He'd changed out of his suit, looking more familiar in his usual faded blue jeans, T-shirt and work boots. His long, lean legs were stretched out slightly in front of him as he leaned against the pier's railing, the ocean at his back. And, God, his eyes…she liked his watchful, heated gaze far too much for comfort. She had no idea why he was here, but as long as he stared, she was staring back.

So screw it.

Flip him the bird or crook her finger? Oh, the choices… Grinning, she flipped him the bird. He tipped his head in silent acknowledgment and then slipped away into the shadows.

She pushed down the strange pang of disappointment. She might not *like* Cal, but baiting him was almost as much fun as eating taffy and riding the swings. He had better things to do than stand there and watch her. Of course.

She'd been kissing distance from him that night at Big Petey's, and the closeness had made an impression. That was all these residual feelings were. Because kissing Cal— or doing anything else with the man—would be a recipe for disaster. His hot body came with an arrogant, take-charge attitude she didn't need in her life. She'd win their bet and thumb her nose at him. So what if she'd imagined the man doing a Chippendales routine at her own personal direction? Just because he'd have to take orders from her didn't mean she had to *give* him any orders. She certainly hadn't planned on actually getting into bed with him.

Lenny bellowed for last-takers, and she tightened her fingers on the chains connecting her swing to the ride. The anticipation of waiting to start was almost as good as the ride itself. As the music swirled and blared, the swing dipped and swayed as someone else sat down beside her. Nope. No way. She always rode alone.

She turned her head—although how she was going to protest sharing a public ride with single seats for solo riders, she didn't know—and Cal settled onto the seat beside her. She couldn't remember the last time Cal had ridden the swings. Or the first time, for that matter.

"I could be saving that seat," she pointed out through a mouthful of candy.

He raised a brow. She *hated* when he did that. The gesture always, always preceded his busting her. Sure enough…

"For whom?"

He reached out a thumb and rubbed at the sticky corner of her mouth. Oops. She was wearing her guilty pleasure on her face. At least he hadn't licked his finger first. Ignoring the rasp of his callused skin against hers, she pulled away from his touch. He was also far too literal. "I didn't say I *was*."

"Just that you could be," he agreed. "Which you're not. So fair game."

"Since when do you ride the swings?"

"Maybe I'm trying something different." His eyes met hers in silent challenge, and she wondered if her comment about his predictability had stung the other night.

Lenny was making final rounds, collecting tickets and

checking the safety harnesses. If tonight were her lucky night, Cal wouldn't have one. Of course, since he was never impulsive, he undoubtedly did.

Lenny paused.

Cal handed over his ticket.

So not her night.

A minute later the ride started, the familiar music drowning out the chatter of the pier's crowds. The lights flashed a riff of rainbow shades, and Discovery Island melted into a colorful blur as they rose up off the ground. She loved this. The sensation was almost as good as platform diving had been. She could—again, almost—pretend she was flying.

Cal ruined it by opening his mouth.

"Good job today," he said. Instead of looking out at the island, he was staring at her again. Cal was always annoyingly fair.

"You, too," she admitted grudgingly. Because it was true, darn it. He *had* done a good job and it worried her. She really, really needed the contract, and Cal might be the person who stopped her from getting it.

The ride whirled up, gravity and centrifugal force working their magic as the swings swung out in a wide arc. She'd sat on the inside because she really hadn't expected company, and he outweighed her. He braced himself as the ride turned, but his thigh pressed against hers. The world spun out of focus, and she couldn't hold back the laughter anymore. Cal's weight changed the swing's pitch but not in a bad way. On the next turn, which came faster and higher, he slid into her—the man had no choice—and she leaned forward.

"There's Deep Dive." She leaned forward and pointed to his shop.

PIPER LIVED ON the edge.

Literally.

Cal wrapped a hand around the back of her neck and gently tugged until she wasn't quite so close to the edge of the seat. The ride had a safety harness, a set of thin chains, which struck Cal as more ornamental than functional. The ride's designers had clearly bet on gravity keeping riders in their places. Equally obvious, they'd never planned on Piper. She'd once debated the feasibility of jumping from the ride, when it swung out over the ocean at its highest point, and hitting the water.

He'd never know for certain whether she'd have gone through with the plan or not, but he'd watched her like a hawk for the rest of the summer until she'd gone back to the mainland with her family. She'd accused him of being an old grandfather. He'd countered that she'd had a death wish.

Her legs extended in front of her as their swing whirled into the next turn, and she threw her arms over her head, shrieking happily. Her right knee didn't quite straighten all the way, the ridge of scar tissue there a visible reminder that some things in life hadn't worked out for Piper. On the other hand, while the accident had put an end to her diving career, she didn't seem to be in mourning.

Instead, she'd moved on.

Or moved back. Cal wasn't sure which. All he knew was that he was off balance in more ways than one, which was pretty much what always happened when he was around Piper.

They needed to let go of this ridiculous bet. It was a stupid idea and unprofessional. He had no idea why he'd agreed to it in the first place, except that when he was around Piper, things seemed to happen. That was part of the problem.

At least he had a captive audience. She couldn't run away from him now. "About our bet—"

"You can't renege," she said. "Look, you can see my boat."

"Piper—"

"That's my name." She slid a sideways glance at him he couldn't read. Too bad Piper didn't come with an instruction manual. Or an off switch.

"We can't do the bet," he said firmly. He knew what happened when he gave Piper so much as an inch.

"You agreed," she countered, every bit as stubborn as he remembered. The years hadn't softened her up any. Or taught her to be reasonable.

He braced as the ride spun higher and the swings arced out into the air. Squashing Piper hadn't been part of his plan. "Cut me some slack."

"Nope," she said. "No way. You were my childhood nemesis. You never went easy on me once."

Her body curved into the turn, and she threw her arms up again with another whoop, taking at least a year off his life as her butt lifted off the seat. He anchored her with an arm around her waist, feeling the warmth of her beneath the thin cotton top. She looked sweet and sexy, both of which were misleading. He had no idea what game Piper was playing with him, but she'd never shown the slightest awareness of him as a man. Or sweetness. Stubborn, fierce, competitive—Piper was all of those. Sweet, however, was not part of her vocabulary.

He didn't even like sweet.

He tucked her bag of candy into his pocket before it flew away. See? Nothing but trouble.

"We'll renegotiate," he stated firmly.

"Cheater," she said, a small smile curling her lips, and

the delight in her voice matched the grin on her face. "You're a cheater, Cal Brennan."

He had no idea what she was talking about. Up, down, sideways. He never knew where he stood with Piper, other than on her shit list. He seemed to have a permanent place there. But that was Piper. She was confusing, annoying and definitely…sexy? It had to be a residual from seeing her bare breasts the other day.

Her spectacular, beautiful, completely naked breasts.

He could feel an answering grin tugging at the corner of his mouth. "Piper," he crooned. "You're not making any sense."

And…his words were the match to her tinder.

"Shut up," she snapped. "And hold on."

She muttered something else he couldn't quite catch— but she'd always had a potty mouth, so he could make an educated guess—and then hooked a finger in the front of his T-shirt, dragging him toward her. He could have stopped her. He was bigger, and he outweighed her by at least eighty pounds. And yet he leaned obediently toward her. Another first for him.

The ride lurched into its final, lightning-quick round, the music building to a deafening roar. His stomach lurched right along, and Piper laughed, her face glowing. She'd always loved riding this monstrosity. He was close enough now to see the paler gold ring in her brown gaze and the freckle by the corner of one eye.

Her hands bunched in his shirt, knuckles brushing his skin, the metal of the dog tags he wore to remember. He had no idea what she was up to. Piper was one surprise after another. She'd never been prone to violence, though, so he figured he'd stay safely in the swing.

She slid over. Up. Working the swing and gravity and

God knew what else until her butt was planted firmly in his lap. *Surprise.*

"Piper—" Her name came out sterner than he'd intended. A warning, because not everything had to be a game between them.

"Shh," she whispered, her eyes twinkling. "I'm working on a safety violation here."

She pressed her mouth against his, and his arms snapped around her, anchoring her. Because they were turning, whirling, and he didn't want her flying out of the swing. Nope. He didn't want her hurt, even if he wasn't sure what else he *did* want.

Her mouth was a wicked surprise, her lips soft and giving as they brushed his. Slightly sticky, too, from the taffy, but he could work with that. He'd never thought of Piper as sweet before tonight—in fact, he tried hard to *not* think about her because he'd suspected danger years ago—but the sugar glossing her lips tempted him to have just a taste of her.

"Wow, Cal." She didn't sound pissed off, which was a pleasant change from her usual mood.

Was that a "yes, do it again"? With his tongue, he traced the line where her lips met, his hands curving into the small of her back, his fingers skimming bare skin where her shirt had ridden up. Definitely a "yes, do it again" from him.

She kissed him and the soft contact was all it took to set his head spinning more wildly than the swings. Just like that, he forgot they didn't like each other and that they were, in fact, competing for the same job. Her lips brushed his, teasing and candy sweet, and his pulse hammered out of control.

Piper was kissing him.

It should have seemed strange or awkward, but somehow, all her touch felt like to him was right. He'd known her for years and never imagined doing this. She pressed into him, centrifugal force pinning her against his chest as the ride swung them briefly out over the ocean, but his arm around her waist kept her there when the ride evened out.

Piper kissed with her eyes open. The look on her face was intent, fierce and more than a little puzzled. That made two of them. Her ponytail flew out behind her as the swings turned, curly strands escaping every which way. The pink flush on her cheeks had nothing to do with makeup. With Piper, what you saw was what you got.

He only wished he knew why she wanted to kiss him.

Curiosity got the better of him, however, so he gently ran his fingers down her eyes, coaxing her to shut them. He couldn't turn his head off with her staring at him. Couldn't lose himself in her. She drove him crazy, but right now kissing her was absolutely what he wanted to be doing, so he angled his mouth over hers, taking control of it.

She whispered his name as he kissed her slowly, deeply, slipping inside her mouth and swallowing the small hums of sound she made. She curled tighter against him and he held on, as if letting go suddenly wasn't an option and not just because she might fly off the swing. She tasted like saltwater taffy and sunlight, all the good things in life. She didn't do this any more quietly than she did anything, however. She made noise. Lots and lots of noise. Hums and groans, gasps and a sexy whimper that made him wish they were anywhere but in public.

Threading a hand through her hair, he cupped her head. She didn't pull away, just moaned, and the raw sound jolted through him, so he kissed her some more.

The ride slowed.

He lifted his head. She pulled back, sliding out of his lap. The swing coasted lower and lower, momentum lost, the Pleasure Pier coming into focus. He might as well have posted a picture on Facebook, because the entire resident population of Discovery Island would know about the kiss before tomorrow morning. *Way to go, sailor.*

His feet bumped the ground, and Lenny immediately headed their way, a big grin splitting his face.

"I should charge you double," the old man snorted.

Piper laughed, snagging her bag of taffy from Cal's pocket. "Like you haven't seen riders kiss before."

She didn't deny what had happened, didn't seem bothered at all. No, he was the only one who felt off balance. On the other hand—he grinned as Lenny unhooked their swing to let them out—winning, and losing, had never looked so good. He wanted the contract *and* the woman— winner take all.

"I'm looking forward to winning our bet," she said throatily. Then she hopped down with a jaunty, "See you," and sashayed down the pier.

Right. The bet he'd been so determined to call off...and that he now had every intention of winning, because holding Piper in his arms for a night suddenly sounded a whole letter better—not to mention hotter—than any contract.

6

APPARENTLY, SHE DIDN'T have to like someone in order to kiss him. Piper's brain had insisted on replaying last night's embrace over and over, much to the delight of other body parts. She'd had no idea Cal kissed so well. Sure, the outward package was hot as hell, but she'd assumed his arrogant attitude would translate into his kisses, as well. Big mistake. He'd been confident and knowing, but there had also been a careful tenderness in the way he cupped her head and worked his mouth over hers and… She had to stop thinking about it. It had been one kiss. She'd initiated. He'd closed.

And the encounter had kept her up all night.

Big mistake.

Cal drove her crazy. He was cocky, too sure of himself and bossy. From the moment they'd met as kids, he'd made it his life's mission to oppose her any and every way he could. Now he had the Fiesta contract in his sights, and if she was very honest with herself, he had as good a chance of winning as she did. She didn't like to lose. Who did? So, no, it wasn't surprising she didn't *like* Cal Brennan.

Cal didn't wear his thoughts and his emotions on his face, but he'd made those sexy, growly noises, so that had to be a positive sign, right? He kissed with his eyes closed, and he had impossibly long eyelashes. When she'd snuck a peek, he'd seemed both hungry and determined. And the touch of his callused fingers… Well, letting go of Cal had been surprisingly difficult.

She eyed the hotel. The cruise ship execs had unexpectedly scheduled a meeting for this afternoon, claiming they had a decision to share, and her new policy was no more kisses until she won. She needed to focus on getting the contract—not on his broad shoulders or sexy presence. Cal was a take-charge kind of man and alpha to the core, so waiting guaranteed she didn't lose control of the situation. Win, and she'd have Cal to herself on her own terms for one hot night. Seeing him give up his tightly honed control was simply a bonus. Cal wasn't the kind of man who took orders in bed—but for one night, he'd take them from her. Her big, bad rescue swimmer wouldn't like it at all, but too darned bad. He'd be all *hers*.

She couldn't wait.

Right on cue, a certain sexy SEAL rode up on his motorcycle. She had a moment to wonder where he was coming from—because his dive shop was right around the corner—but maybe he'd been out at the Brennan place. His family lived on Discovery Island year-round and had an enormous, rambling old house a couple of miles outside town. The home sported the kind of cheerful, shabby chic she'd seen on the pages of various magazines and was a far cry from her own family's summer cabin. Her cabin was a euphemism for "four walls held together with baling wire and duct tape." She'd probably wake up in the ocean one day.

Since she'd spent the morning doing the books at Dream Big and Dive, she'd been just around the corner, and she'd walked. Which—she shot a glance at her sandals with their three-inch heels—had been a stupid thing to do. Her knee would hurt like the devil later tonight, but she'd chosen the shoes because right now she needed to feel sexy. Powerful.

Cal should have looked out of place wearing a suit and straddling a motorcycle, but he didn't. He also probably had another PowerPoint slide presentation, which he'd use to wow the assembled minions, in the messenger bag thrown over his shoulder. She hadn't slept well, which she blamed on Cal. If he hadn't been such a good kisser, she wouldn't be gritty-eyed from all the tossing and turning she'd done. She headed for the door. The sooner the meeting started, the sooner she could win the contract and put all this behind her.

"Ignoring me?" The knowing rasp of his voice almost had her pausing.

Almost.

The truth was: absolutely. She didn't know what she'd been thinking when she'd kissed him. And the blame rested solely on her shoulders. As did their bet, when she thought about it. Whatever. Shaking Cal out of his complacency was practically a public service.

Kissing him had nothing to do with how he'd made her feel.

Absolutely nothing at all... *Liar, liar, pants on fire,* the voice in her head chanted, and her libido nodded along happily. Darn it. This was not supposed to be happening. She wasn't supposed to be feeling anything for Cal other than a little friendly competition. She didn't need things to change.

"Definitely ignoring me." Warm male hands cupped her shoulders, halting her in her tracks. A little zing shot through her as his breath gusted past her ear.

"Apparently, I'm not succeeding." She reached for the door, but he beat her to it.

"You're losing the battle," he agreed cheerfully and pushed the door open, motioning her to go through first.

She considered standing there on the sidewalk, but Cal was stubborn. Since he had the door open, he'd probably stand there until hell froze over or she walked away. And walking away meant giving up on the contract, which wasn't happening, either.

She brushed past him into the hotel, trying to ignore the way the accidental touch brought the hard muscles of his arm to her attention. The door slammed shut behind her, and Cal fell into step beside her, easily matching her pace. Of course, he wasn't wearing heels.

"I take it this means you don't want to talk about last night."

She made a shut-up-now gesture, because, *hello,* they were in the hotel's very public lobby, and they both had to live on the island. She knew Cal's mother. Amy Brennan loved her sons, Cal included, but she also lived to see them married off and reproducing. Cal was the most stubborn holdout of her three sons, so if Mrs. Brennan believed there was any chance Piper and Cal were getting together... Nope. Not happening. Piper was still hoping no photographic evidence of last night's embrace would show up on Facebook.

"You kissed me," Cal pointed out cheerfully, punching the button for the elevator. He looked down at her feet. "I assume we're not taking the stairs, since you're wearing those shoes."

"What's wrong with my shoes?"

"Absolutely nothing," he said. "But I am wondering how you manage to walk in them. Doesn't your knee bother you?"

She wasn't talking about her knee. "My knee is none of your business," she gritted out. The hotel had to have the slowest elevators known to humankind. She'd take the stairs, but Cal was, of course, right. Her feet hurt, her knee throbbed, and if it had been anything other than a business meeting, she'd have toed off the shoes and swapped them for the flip-flops in her tote bag.

"Actually, your knee kind of is my business."

The elevator dinged, the doors slid open and she limped inside. Unfortunately, like always, Cal was right on her heels. He held the door with one large hand and then reached around her to press the button for the third floor.

The doors shut, making her uncomfortably aware the space was too small for the both of them. Plus, all her elevator fantasies rushed unbidden to the forefront of her head.

Cal filled up all the available space, big and sure, but she still wasn't discussing her knee with him. After all, every possible angle of the injury had already been discussed in the national media. When it had become clear she wouldn't be resuming her platform-diving career, the media had run stories about the accident and her broken dreams. She preferred not to relive those moments.

Move ahead.

Don't look back.

If she could change that day, she would. But life didn't pass out do overs, and Cal had saved her life. The truth rankled, if she was being honest. She'd always stood on her own two feet, always pulled herself out of the water, no matter how hard or badly she hit. Except for that one afternoon when she'd needed Cal to do it. Of course, there were worse things than having to say thank you. Things like being *dead*. So even if she wished she'd gotten herself out of trouble, she still appreciated everything Cal had done.

"Third floor?" she asked, ignoring the fact that since

he'd punched the button, it was clearly their destination. Cal never got the details wrong.

"Yeah." He settled in on the other side of the elevator as if she'd never sat on his lap last night or made free with his body. "So, how is your knee?"

"Better." She owed him that much. "Stiff sometimes, and it can only take so much stress before it buckles. I appreciate what you did for me that day."

She did, too, even if she would prefer not to talk about it.

This wasn't the first time she'd thanked him—although, admittedly, it was only the second because, hey, she had her limits—and he once again shrugged off her thanks, as if she'd expressed her appreciation for a cut in line or a cup of coffee. Clearly, in Cal's world, a rescue was just all in a day's work, no matter how much his rescue had meant to her. He dropped his gaze to her knee. For one charged moment, she thought he'd reach out and touch her there.

"So no more platform diving?"

No, and the truth still stung. "The knee can't handle the hurdle. As soon as I push off, it buckles. I couldn't get the air height to be competitive."

"And being competitive mattered most?"

Pretty much. Piper's family competed. In the pool, on the ring or on the field, the Clarks competed and they won. Her parents didn't know what to make of her newfound desire to own a dive shop. Her brothers were simply, fiercely, adamantly protective. Moving to the island and temporarily putting some ocean between her and them had been the only way to avoid suffocating. She'd had a career-ending injury, not a deathblow, but they had a hard time seeing it that way. While she appreciated the open offer of a job on the ranch, it wasn't what she wanted for herself.

"I didn't want to climb the tower and dive, knowing I'd

score dead last in every meet. Plus, I would have been cut from the team after one season anyhow."

So she'd left.

"I tried," he said abruptly. "I did everything I could think of to miss hitting the Jet Ski."

Cal had driven his motorboat into the breakwater, trying to avoid the crash. If he hadn't... Well, the alternative was one more thing on the list of things she didn't think about. She hadn't known he blamed himself in any way for the accident. That was why these things were called accidents and not on-purposes.

"I know," she said, because she did.

"Jesus, Piper. You shouldn't have been out there. You knew better."

And there it was...the lecture he'd probably been storing up for the past five years. She didn't want to hear it now any more than she had back then, when he'd shown up in her hospital room to hear her awkward if heartfelt thanks. She was an adult, not a child he could scold.

"I did. What I did *not* know was that Lance had spent the morning at the bar taste-testing margaritas. If I had, I wouldn't have gone near a Jet Ski with him. I'm not stupid."

The elevator dinged and the doors opened. She was taking the stairs after this meeting. He stepped forward, ever the gentleman, and held the door for her. Since arguing over his good manners would only point out her lack of the same, she started forward.

"Piper." Had his mouth brushed her ear?

She kept on moving. That was the game plan, both for today and for her life.

"I never thought you were stupid, okay? Just—" He ran a frustrated hand over his head.

"Impetuous? Stubborn? Had a mind of my own?" She

gave him the list over her shoulder, still heading toward the conference room. "Check, check and check, big guy. Don't feel sorry for me, though, because I'm about to kick your butt in there and score your contract."

HE'D NEVER ONCE felt sorry for Piper. Not when he'd dived beneath the surface, searching desperately for her body. Not when he'd brought her up, bleeding and unconscious. Not when his mother had mentioned how sweet Piper Clark would never dive competitively again. He'd felt plenty of emotions—anger, frustration, worry and concern heading the list—but pity wasn't one of them. Her strength defied feeling sorry for her because she'd already picked herself up and forged ahead.

She wore another business-casual number today: a hot-pink shirtdress that—once again—stopped well north of her knees. The neck was unbuttoned low enough to reveal a chunky necklace, some kind of beaded flower thing studded with sparkling stones. He was 100 percent certain he'd never seen a flower like that in nature.

She didn't look back at him after she delivered her ultimatum, just sashayed down the hall, away from him, leaving him to admire the sassy hitch to her walk. She'd never asked for pity or even a break. After the accident and their uncomfortable meet and greet in her hospital room, he'd given her some space because it seemed like the whole world had been all over her, wanting to know how she felt about losing her berth on the national diving team. Piper had been born to compete, and she hadn't even had the chance. Lance's criminal decision to drink and drive had guaranteed that, and the brief prison sentence the man had earned couldn't possibly begin to atone for what she'd lost.

The trash talking and competitiveness covered up something else.

He followed her into the room. Part of him actually wanted her to win, which was stupid because he needed the cruise line's business if he wanted to expand Deep Dive's offerings and bring more veterans on board to help out. Piper, however, clearly didn't feel like throwing the contest in his favor. He didn't think it was the chemistry they had between them that made him feel like handing her the win. He hoped.

Ten minutes later, he wasn't sure what to think. He stared at Sal Britten, who'd just delivered his bad news as though it was some kind of trophy.

"So," the man concluded, "We're not sure which direction we want to go in. You're both equally strong candidates, and to be honest, the competition came down to you two. The other applicants weren't even close. One of you is earning the contract, but we're not ready to make a decision today."

Translation: the guy couldn't make up his mind.

Cal hated indecisiveness. From the way Piper practically vibrated on her chair beside him, for once she was in agreement with him.

"We'll have a second round of competition," Sal continued, oblivious to the tension in the room, "with just the two of you competing. We're asking you to pick two dives from your sample programs, something new and innovative our cruisers won't have done before. Then you'll take us out, walk us through them. Since you'll be leading the program, we'd like to see how you work in the field and how well you can bring another dive master up to speed, as sometimes one of the ship's dive masters may be accompanying you. We'll do a morning dive, followed by a surface interval and then we'll finish off in the afternoon."

Hell. Cal had one week to wrestle through his unreasonable reaction to submerging, and that was if he and Piper could actually work together without killing each other. He wanted to believe his diving was possible—he wasn't stupid enough to bet they could cooperate—but…yeah. He could guess the odds. Piper had won and she didn't even know it. He slid a sidewise glance at her.

She blinked, the only sign she hadn't been expecting the news other than that betraying twitch in her seat. She was good.

"Let me see if I've got this straight." She sounded calm. Collected. This was going to be prime. "You want us to make a second pitch. In the water. And you want us to work together."

The cruise ship guy beamed. "Exactly. We can see for ourselves exactly how you'd lead a group. It's perfect."

She narrowed her eyes. "But nobody wins the contract today."

Sal nodded happily, as if he expected Piper to agree wholeheartedly. Clearly, he hadn't done his homework on her.

"In fact, we both *lose.*"

Sal suddenly looked like a deer in the headlights. Cal stepped in before Piper said something to completely torpedo her chances. After all, he wanted this to be an equal competition. Although, if he was truly interested in being fair, a little voice whispered, he'd pull out now. Unfortunately, the chance to needle Piper was too tempting.

"I'm happy to put something together for you. I'm sure Piper here feels the same way."

Yep. She felt *exactly* the way he did. Her pretty little heel ground into his foot beneath the table. She'd apparently remembered he wasn't wearing work boots today. Gently, he hooked a foot around hers.

"Piper?" He shot her a smile and knocked her foot off his. "Are you in?"

"You bet." She sounded all prickly, though.

He loved hearing it. It meant she was paying attention to him, that he'd gotten her riled up good. He didn't know why he enjoyed making her mad…but he always had. From the first time they'd met—which had been at a particularly memorable picnic where Piper had "accidentally" upended her sweet tea in his lap and then jumped off a twenty-foot ledge and into the ocean with her brothers—to, well, just about every encounter they'd had, they'd fought. Except for last night on the swing ride. He didn't know why he and Piper had reacted so strongly to each other, but the chemistry thing probably had something to do with it.

So he stood up, collected his gear and exchanged a round of hearty handshakes with the cruise ship executives. Piper worked the room beside him, clearly determined not to cede him an inch.

In step, they went out into the hallway. The hotel simply wasn't big enough to accommodate a mass exodus of five people. Cal hung back while the executive crowd squashed into the elevator. Piper hesitated but then waved them on. Standing butt to groin with the people you wanted to do business with wouldn't make doing business any easier. There were some things he simply didn't want to know. Apparently, he and Piper had finally found common ground. He grinned.

She leaned back against the wall and made a small, shooing motion with her hand. "You run along, too."

He wasn't sure how she intended him to leave—the elevator had barely begun to make its downward descent and he wasn't jumping out of any windows just to oblige her—so he settled for staring her down. He wasn't going anywhere, and the sooner she accepted his presence, the better. It would have helped if he knew why he'd glued himself to her side, but he didn't. He'd walked her in. He'd walk her out. It was that simple. Plus, it bugged her, which was an excellent fringe benefit.

"We have to work together," he pointed out. "Cooperating means we're going to have to share air space at some point."

"You really think we can work together?" She met him glare for glare, hands propped on her hips. The move drew his attention to the drawstring waist of her dress. She'd tied the narrow cord into a perky bow. One tug, and he'd bet she'd come unwrapped like the best of Christmas presents.

Whoa. Down, boy.

He muttered something under his breath. Nothing about today had gone as planned. Apparently, miracles still happened, however, because she looked away and shrugged.

"I have my doubts." She toed off her shoes with a little groan of relief that shot straight to his groin because he had to imagine she'd make the same sexy sounds in bed. Sex clearly wasn't on her mind, however, because she fished in her bag and produced a pair of battered neon-pink flip-flops she slipped onto her bare feet. "So much better. I'm taking the stairs."

He stared at her toes. She dropped her heels into her bag.

"You don't want to wait for the next car?" His voice sounded husky. This was Piper, he reminded himself. Letting her star in his erotic fantasies would make working with her even more complicated.

She gave him a look he couldn't decipher—other than the absolutely-not portion of it—and opened the door to the stairwell. They were apparently taking the stairs.

He strode after her because it was hurry up or get left behind. Piper was a woman on a mission. She tackled the steps with the determination his sisters used on a new gallon of ice cream. The soles of her flip-flops slapped against the bottom of her feet. She sure was in a hurry to get somewhere.

"There a fire someplace?" he asked, settling in by her side. Having longer legs was an advantage.

"I can't believe they couldn't choose," she burst out, ignoring his question.

"Life's a bitch," he agreed. Her hair brushed his shoulder as she stomped across the landing. Their footsteps echoed in the stairwell loudly enough to be heard halfway to China.

She stopped abruptly and he almost body slammed her. Thank God for instincts honed by military training. He snagged the handrail and waited.

"You didn't win," she said, sounding absolutely sure of herself.

"Neither did you," he snapped. "Does the lack of a clearcut winner from today's meeting bother you?"

She pursed her lips. He wanted to smooth out the crinkle with his finger. Or his tongue. Apparently, he wasn't picky.

Piper, he reminded himself.

She'd probably bite his finger off. He didn't kid himself. Whatever twisted reason had prompted her to suggest the bet, it wasn't because she was attracted to him. Knowing her, it was a power play or some other complicated move in this game she insisted on playing with him. He was the only one who had the urge to change the rules.

"We had a bet. Not knowing who the winner is doesn't bother you?" she demanded, answering his question with one of her own.

It absolutely did. Piper was a sensual temptation, and he found it harder and harder to resist her. He also enjoyed beating her, if only because it made her so adorably mad. That probably wasn't what she wanted to hear right now, however.

He opened his mouth and she cocked a hand on her hip. Waiting for him to admit that, yes, he enjoyed competing with her. Fighting with her. Doing…other things with her. The words that came out of his mouth, however, weren't part of any master plan to win the Fiesta contract.

"If we're talking about the bet, it's safe to say we both lost."

She blinked once before regrouping.

"Good." She glared up at him, stepping into him and backing him up against the stairwell's wall. He loved the way she crowded him. "Because you owe me and I plan on collecting."

The erotic jolt that went through him should have warned him. Whatever his head thought, his body didn't see Piper as the enemy.

7

CARLA, PIPER'S ASSISTANT, part-time dive instructor, gal
Friday and supplier of oatmeal chocolate chip cookies,
looked up when Piper slammed into the dive shop, the door
rattling in its frame. The woman was a gem, and Piper
worried sometimes that she would head out for greener
pastures—or places with more challenging dive sites. So
far, however, Carla had stayed put and Piper was grateful.
When Carla raised an inquiring brow, Piper flipped the
open sign to closed. It wasn't like they were busy anyhow.

Which was part of the problem. The darn economy followed by a bad summer storm had definitely put a dent
in their business. In the wake of the storm, several cruise
ships had skipped the island altogether, and the island's
hotels had been hit by a second storm of cancellations.
Discovery Island had scrambled to clean up and make re-
pairs quickly, but still, all of those things took time—and
dive bookings had been drastically reduced.

Carla had screwed her blond hair up on top of her head
in a messy bun anchored by a flotilla of pencils. Small
curls flew every which way, giving the woman a deceptively cute appeal. Carla was as lethal as a shark. She held

up a bottle of sparkling apple cider, thumb poised to pop the cap off. "Are we celebrating? Did you kick Cal's butt?"

Piper shook her head and tossed her heels across the room. So much for making a powerful statement at the Fiesta meeting.

"Commiserating. Shoot." Carla poured cider into paper cups, passed one to Piper and took a swig. "We need alcohol. Margaritas. These bubbles aren't commiseration material."

Piper was in full agreement with her, but surely something would occur to her. There was always a way to rescue a bad dive.

"We tied. We both lost. Take your pick."

Carla muttered something, and Piper pointed toward the swear jar stashed underneath the counter. They'd had plenty of conversations about not cursing like a trucker in the workplace, as the Mason jar full of quarters testified. Piper was just as guilty in that department as Carla. The local library would be able to afford an addition when they made their donation.

"We didn't get the contract." Carla fished a quarter out of her pocket and added it to their collection.

"Not yet." Piper took a drink. The cider was warm, and alcohol was definitely called for in this situation. "But we will."

She gave Carla the highlights as she ducked into the backroom and switched her business casual for a pair of denim cutoffs and a tank top, restoring the flip-flops when she was dressed. Her feet practically cried in relief, even as her knee gave a warning throb.

"Typical guys. They can't choose between you and Cal, so they offer to date both of you before committing."

"There was a woman executive," Piper pointed out in the interests of fairness when she came back out front.

Carla finished her cup and eyed the bottle. "That stuff is definitely no substitute for the real thing."

"It was cheap." And she was out of cash unless she robbed the swear jar, a low to which she had so far refused to sink. Groceries for the month were going to be noodles and whatever was kicking around in the pantry, unless she actually used Cal's hundred bucks.

"So, Cal Brennan is still the competition?"

"Unfortunately."

Carla settled back, waving her cup. "Why unfortunately?"

"He's good," Piper said morosely, hopping up onto the counter. "Really good. He had them eating out of the palm of his hand as he walked them through imaginary adventure dives. They were practically salivating at the thought of exploring caves and training like a U.S. Navy SEAL."

Cal had had her hanging on his every word, too, although only partly because adventure diving was precisely the kind of thing she'd enjoy. Most of her attention span had had everything to do with the hot SEAL doing the presenting. The sensation of his eyes moving over her body gave her the kind of feeling she got when was diving or jumping. An adrenaline rush, followed by a familiar quiver.

No quivering.

"You'll win." Carla sounded certain. "Your dives are fun. Not everything has to be a mental marathon."

Piper appreciated the vote of confidence.

"So, what are the next steps?"

"I take them out on a sample dive program. I'll do a few dry runs this week and next. Make sure I'm ready to go and there's no room for improvement."

Carla reached up and knocked her paper cup against Piper's. "Cal won't know what hit him."

"He probably won't mind," she said. She'd always enjoyed a good competitor, but Cal was in a league of his own. Not only was he a former U.S. Navy SEAL, but he'd also put together a compelling presentation. *She* wanted to go out diving with him now. Or do other, more personal things. "Plus, he doesn't play fair."

He'd made her go first, although she'd more than evened the playing field by teasing him while he presented.

"He's a Navy SEAL. Doesn't that make him a bona fide hero?"

"In a war zone, yes. In the boardroom? Not so much." Of course, she hadn't been playing fair herself, but she'd keep those details to herself.

"So…" Carla lobbed the paper cup at the recycle bin. "Was it as horrific as my diver last month, who pulled off his wet suit and his speedo in one go? 'Cause the guy was at least sixty pounds overweight and had never heard of manscaping. My eyes are still burning. Cal Brennan is pretty hot."

"It's not a beauty pageant."

"And if it was, you'd win," her assistant said loyally.

Piper performed a pageant wave and wiped away a mock tear. "Thank you. I'll pick up my tiara later."

"But he is, right?"

Unfortunately, Carla was right. "On a scale of one to ten, he's a definite ten. Maybe even an eleven if he keeps his mouth shut."

"Jump him." Carla shrugged. "Get him out of your system."

Piper didn't want to even *think* about how long it had been since she'd had sex. One of the downsides to living on an island with four thousand people was the minuscule size of the dating pool. Casual summer hookups weren't really her thing, which had further limited her options.

Plus, she hadn't dated much in high school or college. A few casual nights out here and there—practice guys, as her teammates called them. She'd been too busy training and competing to do anything else. If she needed a guy for a formal event, she borrowed one from the swim team and called it good. Getting Cal out of her system shouldn't have sounded so appealing.

"I'm not attracted to Cal." Unfortunately, she couldn't summon a shred of proof to back up the statement.

"Not attracted to him? Or you just don't like him? Because you can totally have sex with him without liking him."

True. "Yeah. About that."

"You already did!" Carla fist-pumped. "You go!"

She shot her friend a look. "Absolutely not. There has been no sex. But I may have made a teeny tiny bet with him."

Carla stared at her expectantly. "Don't stop there. Keep talking."

"I may have suggested that the person who loses the Fiesta contract takes orders from the winner for one night. In bed." She thumped her head against the counter. "When will I learn to think before I speak?"

Carla grinned. "Probably never. You might want to plan on winning."

Piper threw her cup at Carla. Unfortunately, she'd done nothing *but* think about Cal and getting him into bed.

"DID YOU KICK butt and take names?" Daeg didn't take his eyes off the trail as he asked his question. When Cal had brought his two former teammates over to the island, they'd vowed to work out together five times a week, putting their bodies through their SEAL paces. They might not be active duty anymore, but they'd stay in fighting form. That was one thing Cal could still control.

Now, four miles into their eight-mile run, he was mentally counting down the seconds until they got to the swimming portion of the day's workout. So far, he'd managed to keep his fear of submerging under wraps. Or, rather, he'd worked around it well enough that Daeg and Tag were pretending they hadn't noticed anything. Eventually, however, they'd point out the obvious. Cal didn't dive. *Ever.*

Daeg had come back to Discovery Island at the beginning of the summer when Cal had put out his call for help and now, two months later, it looked as though the man wasn't going anywhere. He'd rescued Danielle Andrews from the tropical storm that had passed near the island; she'd rescued him from some inner demons of his own. Cal smelled wedding bells in the not-so-distant future. Cal was glad his former teammate had signed on to the dive business permanently, and he was looking forward to bringing more former SEALs out to the island just as soon as he could.

"I made a few calls," he said, keeping his eyes firmly fixed on the path in front of them. "To see if there was anything for sale on Discovery Island. When we bring the new guys on board, we're going to need more gear and possibly a second site to gear up the divers. With the contract, we'd definitely be in the black, and we could expand and start a second dive shop."

He mentioned the name of a business brokerage firm, and Daeg nodded, but didn't slow his pace.

"Did they have anything for you?"

"Yeah. There's at least one place on the island where the half owner is looking to sell his share. I've made an offer, contingent on our getting the Fiesta contract."

Daeg whistled. "Which shop?"

He'd read his email twice to make sure he hadn't mis-read. "Dream Big and Dive," he admitted.

"Piper's place?"

"Apparently it's only half hers." Although he had a pretty good idea how she felt about it. "The broker said she has first position to buy if she can line up the funding, but she hasn't managed to do so, yet."

"Does she know we're bidding to buy out her business partner?"

"Hell, no. I didn't know until today myself," he pointed out. "Plus, there's already another offer on the place that we'd have to beat. Fiesta also wants a hands-on demo in the field before they'll finalize the contracts. I'll tell her when it's a done deal. If she wins, she'll exercise her op-tion to buy anyhow, and it'll be a moot point."

Cal focused on the ground in front of him. The trail was rocky, small pieces of gravel crunching underneath his feet. One misstep, and he'd go over the edge and down the bluff into the horseshoe-shaped bay below. In another hundred yards, the trail would bend back toward the sand, but from here he could still see the southernmost end of Pleasure Pier.

"Four-mile marker," Tag barked, pounding up behind them. Tag ran the way he'd flown rescue choppers, going all out and then coaxing still more speed from some unseen reserve, right when Cal was sure his friend would crash and burn. Every day had gone the same way when the three of them had been part of the Spec Ops rescue team stationed in San Diego. Fighting, swimming, flying—they'd done it all together, and there were no other guys Cal trusted more to have his back.

These guys were the heart and soul of Deep Dive. Sure, there was friendly rivalry, but they'd had each other's backs since Hell Week and their induction into the Navy SEALs.

When he'd left the unit and started the dive program on Discovery Island, he'd wanted to bring his team with him. They got the importance of diving and diving well. If he expanded Deep Dive, he could bring in more veterans. To do that, however, he needed more business and more shop space, hence the offer he'd put in through the broker. Without the Fiesta contract, however, his cash flow would be so tight it would squeak.

They dropped every two miles to bang out push-up reps.

"When?" Daeg grunted, hitting the ground.

Cal dropped and started working smoothly through his own reps. "Two weeks from now."

Fourteen days didn't feel like anywhere near enough time to fix what was wrong with his head. Discovery Island had already used up its quota of miracles when it had avoided a direct hit with a tropical storm earlier in the summer.

"Who's the competition?" Daeg didn't turn his head but picked up the pace of the push-ups. Hell. Cal kicked it up a notch. He wasn't getting out-repped.

"Who said I had competition?"

"Eighty-one." Tag, the overachiever, knocked out a butt-load more than the U.S. Navy's required forty-two push-ups. If he went back to the SEALs, he'd pass the PT exam without breaking a sweat.

Cal snuck a peek at his watch on his way toward the ground. Tag had accomplished his mission-impossible numbers in ninety seconds. Tag rolled smoothly onto his back, sucking in air. Ten seconds left. Cal powered through reps, back straight, hands and feet planted on the ground. "Dream Big and Dive's the last competitor left standing."

Daeg whistled and flopped to the ground. "Eighty-seven. You've got three seconds to concede defeat. Which you might want to think about doing with Piper. She's going to be one unhappy woman."

Defeat wasn't a word any of them knew. Cal finished the last rep, arms burning. "Eighty-nine."

Tag raised an eyebrow. "The form on your last rep was highly questionable. I'm calling it as a does-not-count."

They squabbled amicably for the rest of the two-minute rest period. As soon as Tag called, "Time," they started crunching. Arms crossed over his chest, fingertips on his shoulders, Cal watched the bay come and go from his field of vision.

"You really think Dream Big and Dive can beat us?"

"Not a chance." He had to work through this, but not with a boatload of divers depending on him. Get in the water. Descend. It wasn't complicated. He'd logged thousands of dives.

"Hooyah." Tag jackknifed up smoothly.

"Piper's a world-champion diver." Daeg shot him a glance. "Plus, if Fiesta's passing out points for personality, she's going to give us a run for our money."

"She didn't actually make it to the world championships," Cal pointed out.

"She earned a berth on the team, and she would have gone if her accident hadn't busted up her knee. The media had her pegged as a shoo-in for gold. The cruise ship people will eat her history up."

Probably. "A good story doesn't make her the best fit for the job." He kept his eyes on the harbor and the boats there, bobbing up and down.

Daeg snorted. "Right. It could be a rout."

"A melee. A debacle." Tag rattled synonyms off as if he was channeling a thesaurus.

"Face it." Daeg finished his reps, shoved to his feet and

started running down toward the beach. It was Armageddon time. "You don't know how *not* to compete."

Daeg had a point.

Cal pounded after his buddy, Tag dogging his heels. As soon as they hit the sand, Daeg toed off his shoes and ran into the water.

"To the point and back?"

Tag splashed into the surf. "You bet. Last one back buys the beer."

Half a mile out, half a mile back. One thousand seven hundred and sixty yards, and forty-five minutes.

Damn it. He didn't want to do this. It didn't matter how clear and debris free the water was or that he'd bump into nothing if he went under. Ever since the first five-hundred-yard swim of his SEAL Physical Screening Test, the combat sidestroke had been second nature, as easy as walking or running. He swam and swam well, covering five hundred yards in under twelve minutes and competing against himself to better his time. The stroke kept the body low in the water, which was a plus when the day's mission included bullets flying at him while he swam.

He'd take bullets any day.

He toed off his sneakers and dropped his T-shirt on the sand. Then he walked over to the water's edge. The surf in the bay wasn't bad, the waves cresting at one to two feet. There was a current to fight on the way out to the point, but on the way back, the same current would push him to shore. The problem wasn't the water or the current. It was in his head.

Daeg and Tag ripped cleanly through the water's surface. They swam hard and fast, pushing underwater until their air ran out, then popping to the surface and dropping into the combat sidestroke. He'd bought the beer every night since Tag had named the stakes.

At least he was in the water. He looked down. Up to his ankles. He compromised with his head and waded in. There was no point in agonizing over a dive he couldn't make. Plus, if he hung back much longer, Daeg and Tag would definitely notice his absence.

Pushing off, he started swimming, pulling hard against the current. He kept his head up (*chicken,* his brain accused), his hips sinking correspondingly lower in the water. He was in, he reminded himself. The sooner he touched those rocks on the point, the sooner he could head back, and this would be over for today. The ocean dragged at his lower body. If he dropped his head even a few inches into the water, the resistance would ease up, but not even Armageddon would get his head underwater voluntarily today.

Twenty minutes later, he neared Daeg—who'd started his return trip—as he pulled close to the point. The other man had already touched and turned, switching sides to pull for the shore.

"Don't you get tired of buying?" Daeg's gaze swept over him, but he didn't stop. He was a neat swimmer, almost no splashing from his feet. Cal had a bad feeling his former teammate knew far too much about Cal's predicament. They were both pretending everything was okay, however, which counted for something.

Cal kicked hard for the point, turning in a smooth arc. It would have been faster to somersault and push off the rocks like a competitive pool swimmer but yeah…turning underwater was apparently off-limits to him, as well. As soon as his head went underwater, all hell broke loose in there and he panicked. Pushing down the self-disgust—

he had hours of non-water time in which to revisit it—he slowly turned and headed for shore.

It looked as though he'd be buying the beer again tonight.

8

PIPER KILLED THE motor and coasted toward the dive buoys scattered across the surface of the water. A good dive would clear her head, and yesterday's bombshell from the good folks at Fiesta had certainly gone a long way toward making things muzzy. She needed to focus on the game because there was too much at stake not to give it 100 percent. Or 200 percent. She grinned. Cal wouldn't know what had hit him.

Rose Wall wasn't one of the better-known dive sites dotting the ocean around Discovery Island, but it was one of her favorites. Nice and shallow, the location didn't have a whole lot of currents to trip up a novice diver, and the colors here were gorgeous. The site had earned its name from the gorgeous kelp forest stretching floor to surface. Bright pink-and-orange anemones peeked out through the green fronds, like flowers in an underwater garden.

And…go figure. Her arch nemesis had beaten her to the punch. The *Dive Boat I* bobbed lazily in the water, already tied up to one of the buoys. She'd sent Cal a brief text announcing her intentions of working this dive site into their joint demo. When he hadn't shown up at her boat slip at the time she'd mentioned, however, she'd left without him. Happily and without giving him so much as an extra second, but she'd made the offer.

Working with Cal ranked way down on her to-do list, right there with having a root canal or filing her taxes. He'd want to be in charge. He always did, and if she was being honest, he was good at it. Cal always had a plan, and he had a way of issuing orders that made other people happy to comply. Unfortunately for him, she wasn't other people. Unfortunately for both of them, however, the Fiesta guys had been perfectly clear on one thing. The two of them had to put together a diving demo. Together.

Apparently, Cal wasn't taking the grade school approach of one group member doing all the work and the rest simply scrawling their names on the project when it was time to turn the work in. His being here wasn't a surprise, but as far as she could tell, he was alone. The cardinal rule of diving was no one dived alone. Cal treaded water on the surface, although the dive marker was in the water, indicating a submerged diver. She did a quick scan of his boat and all of the dive tanks were present and accounted for. Something was off, but she couldn't put her finger on it, so she fell back on her old standby. Fighting with him.

"Trying to get the jump on me, Brennan?" She brought the boat in, and Carla snagged the mooring line, tying them up to the buoy and dropping the anchor over the side.

He slicked the water back from his face. "Do I need to define the word *partners* for you?"

He reached the *Feelin' Free* in a few swift strokes, the muscles in his arms flexing as he pulled himself out of the water. Water ran down his chest and over the muscles of his abdomen. How was any woman supposed to ignore all the gorgeousness? Piper herself lacked the willpower. Her brain was too busy trying to imagine him in one of those barely there Speedos favored by the island's European guests. She'd bet it would be a good look for him. Almost as good as the wet look.

He popped his fins off. "The deal was we worked together."

"Which is why you're making yourself at home on my dive boat?"

She yanked her zipper up on her wet suit. She shouldn't be looking at him. So what if he'd turned into a hottie sometime between the age of ten and thirty? He was still Cal, the eternal pain in her butt and the man who thought he could snag the contract she'd worked so hard for.

"You told me to be here," he pointed out, all Mr. Logic.

"At the slip in the marina." She slapped her dive harness on. "Thirty minutes ago."

"You didn't wait for me." Now he sounded amused.

"You were late."

The amused crinkles at the corners of his eyes said he wasn't so sure. "Did you time me?"

Carla snorted behind her but kept her mouth shut. Wise woman.

"You're not in charge, Piper," he said softly.

"Neither are you." Finished gearing up, she switched her attention—or as much of it as she could, at any rate—to checking the gauges on the steel tanks.

He shrugged. "We have to figure this out."

He sounded so calm. So logical. While she, on the other hand, wanted to knock him overboard with one of the dive tanks. He'd been like that for as long as she could remember, always the golden boy, so responsible and mature.

"You coming in?" She made a show of checking his boat. "Oh. Too bad. You seem to be missing a dive buddy. I guess I'll have to get started without you."

He grinned. "Ladies first. I thought we'd established that."

Dive checks complete, she rolled backward over the side of the boat, keeping a hand on her mask. Knees up, she floated to the surface and flashed Carla the okay sign.

As SOON AS Carla entered the water, Piper bent at the waist, then drove her arms over her head, straightening her legs as she stroked downward with her arms. Her fins flashed briefly and then she slipped beneath the surface. No splash. Just here and then gone. Damn if that wasn't Piper all over again.

She was a force of nature.

She'd also made it perfectly clear how she felt about working with him. He didn't know how he felt about it himself, but it was a prerequisite for winning the Fiesta contract, so he'd do it.

He eyeballed the water. Recreational diving had nothing on combat diving. He'd led covert missions to scope enemy beaches and catalog the ocean floor for natural obstacles and land mines that might impede the navy's landing craft. Executed midnight rescue swims that had ended in gunfire. Rappelled out of choppers, and, yeah…there'd been one memorable occasion when he'd almost planted fins first on a shark in the Indian Ocean. A site like Rose Wall shouldn't pose any problem.

But…it did. The smooth surface taunted him. He didn't want to get in and he definitely didn't want to go under. If he couldn't do it, however, he wouldn't win the contract. And that was hardly the worst problem. Nope. Something in his head was broken beyond all repair, and yet he was under the gun to fix it.

Piper's shadow disappeared from his line of sight. The boat suddenly seemed a whole lot emptier now with her gone. Which was what he'd wanted, he reminded himself. He didn't need an audience for this next part. He was a U.S. Navy SEAL: he got in the water and he went under and he did his job. All too often, life and death had ridden on the success of his ops. He'd spent his life rescuing other people from the ocean.

Too bad he was the one who needed rescuing now.

Damn it.

He stood up, tugging his mask down and into place. The boat rocked gently, mockingly, as he took one large step off the side of Piper's boat and let go, exhaling sharply. *One second.* Water rushed over his head as he went under. *Don't think.* BUD/S training included drown-proofing. Arms and legs tied together, he'd voluntarily dropped down into a thirteen-foot pool only to release his air and power back to the surface. Over and over. *Two seconds.* If he could do that repeatedly, he could do this once.

Three seconds.

And yet the panic was there. Some part of him wasn't convinced he wasn't neck-deep in the Indian Ocean, diving in churned-up, debris-filled water while he looked for Lars and came up empty-handed. He'd failed that day.

Hell, he was still failing.

Four seconds.

He broke the surface, tearing the snorkel from his mouth and sucking in long gasps of air. The sunshine and the ocean's flat surface mocked him. No Blackhawk chopper hovered overhead, its rotors churning the water's surface into a blinding froth. No basket. No rope ladder up. Just him and a beginner's dive he couldn't cope with.

He needed to dive. Once he got back into the saddle, everything would be fine. If he had even one good dive under his belt, he'd be closer to fixing the mess he was in.

He had to hold it together. Too bad his body hadn't gotten the memo.

He inhaled slowly, pulling salty air deep into his lungs. Boat oil. Neoprene rubber. *All good things.* Unfortunately, cataloging the scents and smells of the ocean didn't distract his mind from where he was. Worse, the earthy, pungent scent of loose strands of sea kelp floating on the surface reminded him he wasn't really alone in the water. Debris from a tsunami might not choke the slice of the Pacific surrounding Discovery Island, but there was still plenty of stuff to bump into out here.

He dipped his face into the ocean, tipping his head back to drain the water out of his mask. When he looked down through the mask, he spotted Piper and Carla moving gracefully down the anchor line toward the bottom. Rose Wall was a beautiful dive. The site description included a kelp forest and schools of yellowtails. The question was, did he join Piper or did he sit the dive out, bobbing around on the surface like an old woman?

Before he could overthink it, he took another long breath, focusing only on the push of air through his lungs and his rib cage expanding. He dived at a slant, the water pressure on his back driving him down toward the bottom. Seven feet. Eight. Then a piece of seaweed brushed his leg. Or a shark. A goddamned tree. He didn't know what it was, but he felt the electric shock of the unexpected touch through the three-millimeter wet suit. *Hell.* This time, the flashback rolled over him, impossible to ignore. He sucked in water through his snorkel, no longer sure which end was up and which down.

PIPER SANK SLOWLY, feet first, dumping air from the BC as she exhaled. Pinching her nose closed, she breathed out gently until her ears equalized and then started mentally mapping the corals and underwater formations. Getting lost on her way back to the boat wasn't part of her plans. Overhead, an explosion of bubbles marked Cal's entry into the water.

She paused, waiting to see if he'd be joining them. He hadn't indicated any intentions of doing so, but she didn't want to leave him behind or swimming to catch up if he'd changed his mind. What she didn't see, though, was a tank or diving fins. He dipped below the surface briefly, diving in a smooth, clean arc. At seven feet he slowed. At twelve…something happened. She wasn't sure what, but Cal's body jerked and flailed. Grabbing her dive slate, she scrawled a note for Carla.

"He okay?"

Carla pointed toward Cal in silent question, and Piper nodded. Both women watched Cal for a moment. He clawed his way to the surface and then his big, powerful body cut through the water away from her boat in a familiar combat stroke. In the water, Cal had always been all raw power, a sure, confident swimmer. Piper had no difficulties imagining him doing the SEAL thing. His hands never rose above the surface, his legs methodically propelling him through the water and away from the *Feelin' Free*.

Huh.

So, okay, no law said Cal had to dive. He could have brought a dive boat out here because he felt like a swim or wanted to check out the currents firsthand or any number of a dozen things. Despite what she'd said to him, she didn't really believe he was trying to get the jump on her or intended to cut her out of the contract competition. Cal didn't operate that way. He was blunt. He didn't mince words.

His straightforward attitude had also been what had

driven her crazy in the past, because he'd never held back with her. He'd called her irresponsible, impulsive, dangerous.... He'd slapped labels on her so fast that she'd never considered being anything but what he'd called her. Headfirst, feetfirst, any way, as long as she was all in.

She hung in the water as she watched Cal. Hundred-foot-tall columns of green kelp waved lazily toward the surface, strands forming a soft backdrop for the schools of bright orange damselfish. The Rose Wall site was like being in an underwater forest. Plants covered the rocky bottom, clearly visible in the bright light filtering down from the surface. Her bubbles disappeared overhead.

"Ladies first?" Carla scrawled on the tablet and flashed her a grin. Her dive buddy had the worst handwriting known to humankind. She should have been a doctor.

Piper picked up the pencil. "Why didn't he bring his dive buddy?"

Cal's boat sat low in the water, indicating the steel tanks lined up on his deck were full. Another twenty yards into her swim and she spotted his anchor line. He was at the boat now, and she ran her eyes over what she could see. Whatever had happened back there on the surface, he seemed fine now. She could make out the sleek black outline of his wet suit and diving fins. She didn't know what to think. He wasn't wearing a weight belt or harness, so he'd had no intention of diving?

"Free dive?" Carla scrawled back.

Piper shrugged. Maybe she should chalk it up to one of life's little mysteries. Just because Cal usually had a plan didn't mean the man always did. Perhaps he was human, after all. Beside her, Carla started taking pictures. Their plan was to pitch a "hike through an underwater forest," followed by a swim with sea lions, and these pictures would seal the deal.

And yet, as she worked to catalog the site and mentally mapped out the course she'd use with the Fiesta divers next week, Piper kept one eye on Cal, her curiosity killing her. What was he up to? He was a highly trained diver who specialized in extreme dives. This shallow site with its easy currents wasn't his cup of tea, but he should have been down here, swimming circles around her and Carla.

Nope. It was none of her business.

He dived again, a shallow, graceful arc ending fifteen feet beneath the surface. His body bucked and jerked. Cal never panicked. A little water or a faulty snorkel tube? Those kinds of problems were merely a blip on his SEAL radar. She'd heard the stories about Hell Week, a training week all U.S. Navy SEALs went through. Stories included passing out at the bottom of the pool and near drowning.

And yet Cal was in trouble.

She tapped Carla on her shoulder and pointed up. When Carla nodded and flashed her the okay signal, she started her ascent, slowly rotating upward in a circle toward the surface. When she reached fifteen feet, she stopped for a safety check, hanging in the water. Overhead, Cal disappeared. He'd either grown wings or gotten back on board. She counted down three minutes, then moved steadily to the surface. Racing to the top would be a rookie mistake, and she'd already made too many of those around Cal.

As soon as she broke the surface, she motioned for Carla to get back on the *Feelin' Free*. And then hesitated. This had to be one of her stupidest ideas—and she'd had plenty of those. But, instead of getting back on her own boat, she was going to go stick her nose in Cal's business. Make sure he was really okay.

After passing her gear up to Carla, she swam over to

Cal's boat and hauled herself up onto the gunwale, kicking hard. Cal was sprawled in the captain's seat, looking like a pirate. His board shorts rode low on his hips, exposing the tantalizing ridges and shadows of his abdomen. Despite the towel in his hand, water droplets slicked his face and his chest. It really wasn't fair how good he looked.

She swung her legs over the side and watched him.

He didn't look like he was in trouble.

"I think I get to shoot unauthorized boarding parties." He stood up in a smooth rush of power and padded toward her, all lazy, masculine grace.

She made a show of looking around his boat, ignoring the gunwale digging into her butt and the *Feelin' Free*'s motor sputtering to life behind her as Carla got her boat going. "Where's your dive buddy, Brennan?"

He held the towel out to her. "I came out here alone. Apparently, I'm giving you a lift back to the marina."

A free towel was a free towel. She took it and scrubbed at her face. "Way to go breaking the rules. I didn't know you had it in you."

He crouched, sliding his hand around her ankle and tugging off her fins. She felt the curl of his fingers right through her dive bootie.

"What happened down there?" Because something had. She'd watched him jerk frantically toward the surface, and yet she hadn't seen any cause for alarm.

"Nothing happened." His level gaze met hers as he pulled off the bootie and set it on the deck before reaching for her other foot.

"I know what I saw. You got in the water, you dove and…"

"And what?" His tone dared her to complete the sentence. The problem was, she wasn't sure *what* she'd seen. Cal was a master diver and U.S. Navy SEAL. There shouldn't have been too much he couldn't handle, and she'd never seen him panic.

Not once.

And yet what she'd witnessed was suspiciously close to panic.

"You couldn't finish the dive," she said. "You started down and then you surfaced."

He shrugged impatiently, turning back to the boat's control panel. A quick flick of his fingers, and the motor started up.

"I wasn't dressed for diving," he pointed out.

He hadn't geared up. True. And yet she couldn't shake the feeling something was wrong. That she'd overlooked something obvious.

"Nothing went wrong," he said firmly. "I decided against free diving. I had a malfunction."

"Bad snorkel?" She gave him a question of her own.

"Something like that." His dark eyes were unreadable.

She knew prevarication when she heard it. Playing for time, she unzipped her wet suit to her waist, prying her arms out of the Neoprene rubber. She was absurdly glad she'd gone with her favorite bikini top this morning.

"I should make you swim." He sounded tired and that made her feel all melty inside. *No.* Fighting was better. *She* was better at it.

"I'll ride back with you to the marina," she said.

9

THE RIDE BACK to the marina was uneventful. If Piper had been behind the wheel of the *Feelin' Free,* Cal bet she'd have opened up the throttle and raced him every inch of the way. Instead, Carla kept the other motorboat to a nice, steady pace, content to follow Cal's lead.

Piper dropped down onto one of the bench seats where she had a direct line of sight on him. "You want to talk about it?"

He didn't have to ask what "it" was. Piper wasn't blind. She'd clearly seen him struggling on his free dives, and now she was asking the questions he didn't want to answer. He tightened his grasp on the steering wheel and let the speedometer creep up a little.

"There's nothing to discuss," he said, because admitting to the truth was impossible.

"Uh-huh." Piper didn't sound as if she believed him. "The dive didn't work out so well for you."

He shrugged. "We both know you're going to insist on using Rose Wall in our demo. Your text mentioned sea lions, as well. Maybe I'm tired of fighting you on every point, Piper."

She gave him what he was coming to think of as The

Look. "You think? We're oil and water. I'm not sure we've ever agreed on anything."

"Yeah, but I blame you."

She smiled and looked out over the water. Discovery Island's harbor wasn't precisely a bustling hotbed of activity. A few motor launches headed in and out, ferrying visitors who'd plunked down a substantial number of dollars for a charter fishing trip. Piper looked rumpled and relaxed, her hair whipped into salty curls by her dive and the breeze. She'd shoved her wet suit down to her waist and he couldn't help but notice her breasts in her bikini top. Two small pink triangles of fabric cupped her curves.

"You wish," she said.

"You could try agreeing with me," he pointed out. "In fact, you could just try listening. I'm not the bad guy in this picture. I want to give a good demo every bit as much as you do."

Or more. Honestly, he had no idea what to say to her. The five feet separating them on deck might as well have been a million miles. Bridging the distance was impossible.

She sat cross-legged on the seat, arm extended along the gunwale as her body melted into the up and down of the boat. "How are we going to make this work?"

He had no idea.

Bending over, he popped the top on the cooler by his feet and tossed her a bottle of cold water. "We have to put together a program of two dives. We'll use one of yours and then I'll pick a second site."

"We'll pick the second site together," she said firmly.

Her definition of *partner* was closer to *dictator*. "You picked Rose Wall."

"You don't like the site?"

"It's easy," he countered. "We take uncertified divers out there all the time. There's no challenge to it."

"A dive doesn't have to be hard to be worthwhile."

For the next fifteen minutes, they bickered amicably, until the marina came into view. The arguing kept his mind off the dive he hadn't made. *Good.*

As he pulled into the slip, she hopped out onto the dock and helped him tie off. He wanted to say something, but he was out of words. Piper was confident and sure as she went about the business of docking, so even that topic of conversation was out. He turned the boat off and grabbed her gear. She was already padding down the dock to the dunk tank, pushing the damp wet suit down her thighs with a wriggle.

And...wow. The wet suit hit the ground and her pink bikini had his body heating right up. When she bent over and swiped up the wet suit, his blood pressure soared. How did she manage to get under his skin without even trying?

He contemplated that while he rinsed her booties and fins in the freshwater tank at the end of the dock. Beside him, her arm brushing his, she dunked the wet suit.

"Where's Carla?"

She snorted. "Probably closing up the dive shop or giving us space to kill each other."

"Death or permanent injury would make a joint demo hard."

"We fight," she stated matter-of-factly.

True. "We could try *not* fighting," he suggested.

"Yeah. And you could try not giving orders."

"Your shoes are on your boat," he pointed out.

"I'm tough. Walking barefoot isn't going to kill me."

"Uh-huh." She'd say the same thing if she were strolling over hot coals. "Humor me."

"Because it's safer?" There was no missing the gentle tease in her voice.

There was nothing wrong with wanting to keep her from harm. "You want a piggyback instead? You're going to burn your feet on the dock." It was shocking how hot a nail baking in the summer sun could get.

Her eyes narrowed. "The boards can't be that hot, and I weigh a lot more than I did when I was eight."

He plucked her gear out of the rinse tank and folded it neatly into his dunk bag. He pulled on his own T-shirt.

"And that's a good thing."

Her disgruntled huff had him smiling. "Sometimes, honesty isn't your best policy, Cal."

She looked great. He pulled a pair of flip-flops out of his bag and tossed them to her. "Your other choice is to use these."

"News flash. Our feet are *not* the same size."

"Put them on."

"Right." She gave an exasperated sigh but shoved her feet into the flip-flops. He had big feet. She didn't. She also sported a topcoat of bright green nail polish his own feet were missing. Then—yep—four steps in, he heard the moment she kicked the shoes off.

"Busted," he said, stopping. "Choose. Shoes or a lift."

"I'm fine. I'm not going to burn."

He gave her The Look when she picked up her pace. Sure enough, her feet were burning, and they still had a ways to go. "A or B. It's simple, Piper."

"You're truly volunteering to haul my butt from here to my dive shop?"

He considered her question for a moment. "To the boardwalk, yeah. And across the road. I promise not to bite unless you ask me to."

She stopped dead, propping her hands on her hips, legs

apart. Experience had taught him that Piper didn't like ultimatums of any sort.

"I think I can handle you," he said.

And…match to the gasoline. She pointed a finger at the dock. "Fine. Bend down. Squat. Do something to close the distance between us unless you want me to scale you like a monkey on a tree."

It figured certain more southern parts interpreted her words as an invitation. He dropped to one knee. "Climb away."

She twined her arms around his neck, her bare arm brushing his throat. Her position plastered her breasts against his back, the only things between them his cotton T-shirt and her bikini. Then she wrapped her legs around his waist and he stopped thinking.

Just for a moment because…

He stood up, trying to ignore his new view of a pair of long, muscled legs. Piper's legs were bare and sun-kissed, only the ridges of scars on her right knee white. And the sweet, hot heat he felt against the small of his back? *Don't think about it.* Piper's swimsuit drove him crazy. It needed more fabric. Or iron plating.

"Mush," she whispered in his ear.

STUPID. PIPER HAD sworn not to let Cal push her buttons again. And yet here she was, the soles of her feet burning as she bounced up and down on his back like she was four years old or he was the very best kind of pony ride. He'd dared her and she'd caved, when she could have made a mad dash for the end of the dock and a shady spot. Her arm brushed his neck, and she realized the man had soft places, after all.

Two minutes to the end of the dock. Another minute to cross the boardwalk and reach her shop, at which point he unceremoniously dumped her down his back. Piper had no idea three minutes could last so long or that it was even possible to provoke Cal into being less than a gentleman.

Carla looked up from where she was checking gear when Piper ducked inside. "Please tell me you have plans for our resident SEAL?"

Nipping into the backroom, Piper grabbed the clothes she'd left behind. Hanging around Cal in a bikini wasn't her best bet.

"What kind of plans?" she hollered back, shimmying out of the bikini. Panties were a good start, plus it was wear-your-favorite-bra-to-work day, a padded number designed to give her the cleavage God had denied her. Blue jeans, a tank top and her steel-toed boots. That had to be enough armor to keep Cal at bay. Just in case, she shrugged on her flannel shirt because gravel sometimes kicked up on the road.

"Sexy plans," Carla bellowed. They really needed to discuss the concept of an inside voice. The odds of Cal having *not* heard Carla's repartee seemed distinctly low.

She grabbed her tote bag and shoved the wet bikini inside. "I haven't decided."

Liar, her lady parts screamed. *You know exactly what you want to do to him.*

"I could make you a list." Carla moved toward the windows when Piper stepped back into the front room. "Starting with, strip him down. Although I'd leave the dog tags. I love those on my man."

"We're competing for the same business contract." Darn it. Her voice got all soft and husky on the last words.

"You also had a bet," Carla pointed out. "And he lost."

"So did I." As much as it galled her.

"Take advantage of him." Carla shoved her toward the door. "When's the last time you had fun?"

Carla's definition of fun was dangerous, and Piper knew she was wavering. And was lost when Carla popped open the door and leaned out. "Are you as good as you look?"

Cal raised a brow. "I plead the Fifth."

"Right." Carla avoided Piper's attempt to smack her. "Because I promise you that Piper here is."

Cal raised a brow, all masculine amusement. Yep. He knew what Carla was up to.

"Okay." Something inside her broke. Hot and wicked and…right. She strode toward her bike. "Get on."

She gestured toward her Harley. The low-slung orange-and-chrome bike with its powerful engine was her baby. She didn't let just anyone ride with her. She hoped he appreciated the invitation.

"Where are we going?" He didn't move, his feet still planted on her sidewalk. Carla smirked and retreated inside the dive shop. *Wise woman.*

"My house. We'll do it there. If my bike is in front of your house overnight, your mother is bound to drive by and notice."

"It?" He grinned but looked slightly dazed. She wasn't ceding home-court advantage to Cal. Plus, his mother would have them engaged before breakfast. Not that she was planning on sticking around until breakfast.

"You owe me one night. I plan to collect."

A smile tugged at the corner of his mouth. "We both lost."

"Ladies first," she reminded him and tossed him her spare helmet. He caught it by reflex.

Throwing a leg over the bike, she patted the seat behind her. "Get on."

He came over and then paused Yep. Cal was thinking instead of jumping. "Just so I'm clear, what exactly are we doing here?"

"We're having sex." She flipped the key in the Harley's ignition and reached for her own helmet.

Cal swung onto the seat behind her, caging her between his arms. "And we're doing this because...?"

"To get it out of our systems. And because you lost a bet." She gunned the motor and he groaned.

"Hold on."

"I plan to."

CAL WRAPPED HIS arms around Piper's middle. Possibly, he held on a little tighter than necessary. While he considered his less-than-gentlemanly impulse, he tucked his head beside hers, resting his chin on her shoulder. The position gave him a prime view down the front of her shirt and of the black bra with strips of blue lace. The cups pushed her breasts up and he could imagine all sorts of things he'd like to do to her bra, starting with getting her out of it.

Piper's family owned a ramshackle cabin on the water's edge. Fewer than ten minutes after they'd left town, Piper veered off the main road and took them down a gravel driveway, which spit rocks when Piper took the final stretch too fast. She parked hard, killed the engine and slid off the bike.

"Home sweet home."

He tried to remember how long it had been since he'd last stopped by the Clark place. The roof was missing a few more shingles, and the paint had long since peeled off. The yard, however, still sported the same mismatched collection of Adirondack chairs, piled with colorful cushions and surrounded by half-melted tea lights in jars. A bug zapper connected to the house by a frayed electrical cord did its thing overhead. *Jesus*. She was going to cause a fire.

Of course, it wouldn't be the first fire the Clark place had witnessed. In addition to the tamer pursuits of bonfire building and marshmallow roasting (safely down on the beach with a few cubic tons of water on hand), Piper and her brothers had built signal fires in the barbecue after reading a book about Lewis and Clark. They'd also experimented with setting leaves on fire with a magnifying glass, fished birds' nests out of the cottage's stopped-up chimney and practiced their long jump over the fire Piper's dad had built to burn the fallen leaves. *Good times.* It was a miracle any of them had survived.

"Come on." She strode away from the bike, without waiting for him, and made for the door.

He didn't like following like a puppy on a leash. He also didn't know why he was here. He half expected her to turn around, yell "Gotcha," and send him on his way. Since there was no figuring Piper out, he settled for watching her very fine ass lead the way. The worn denim cupped her in all the right places, and so, yeah, maybe he knew *exactly* why he was here. He and Piper were oil and water, but they had chemistry.

When she flicked open the screen door without so much as a pause, however, he was back to seeing red. "You didn't lock the door?"

"It's Discovery Island. We're not a hotbed of urban crime." Piper moved inside, tossing her keys onto the side table and dropping her messenger bag on the floor. Great. Any passing moron could rob her blind just by opening the door and reaching down.

Her place still looked pretty much the same. Slipcovered sofas flanked the stone fireplace, and stacks of books and oil paintings covered every available inch of wall space. Floor-to-ceiling windows gave way to a view of the ocean, and he walked over to them. The dock stretched out into the water, and she had a small slice of beach all to herself. Roses, blue morning glory and wisteria covered every inch of the front porch. If she hadn't reinforced the roof, she'd need to soon.

"So." Piper paused, and for the first time he spied a hint of uncertainty, quickly banished, on her face. He leaned against the wall and waited for her to make the next move in this game they were playing. This was going to be good.

"Where do you want me?" he asked agreeably.

The sun was setting now, lighting up the ocean with color, but the light inside Piper's house was soft and golden. She picked up a sofa cushion and dropped it, sending motes of dust dancing in the sunshine. Her housekeeping skills hadn't improved any over the years.

Piper cursed and he held back a grin. She wasn't getting out of this one with a witty comeback. She'd started something she didn't want to finish and, yeah, watching her squirm was fun. He'd tease a little bit more—because this was *Piper*—and then he'd call Daeg and head back to his own place. He might not have been in the cottage in years, but some things stayed the same. He headed for the hallway.

"Bedroom's down here, right?"

"I need a beer," she said behind him. "Or a margarita."

The grin was unstoppable this time, but he had his back to her and she couldn't see.

Finding her bedroom wasn't hard to do. The cottage had only three bedrooms and, when he opened the doors, two of them were clearly unused. Plus, she'd chosen the room he'd have picked, the one where he could see the ocean from the bed. Piper had left her mark in here, too. The bed had enough height to reenact the Princess and the Pea. Plus, the surface was buried beneath a mountain of useless little throw pillows. Huh. Not what he would have imagined. He cleared a spot and lay down on the bed, legs stretched in front of him and crossed.

The sound of a blender echoed down the hallway. Apparently, Piper had meant one thing tonight. It was margarita time.

"You want me naked?" he hollered.

She ignored him, so he removed his boots and set them on the floor where he could grab them if he had to make a quick retreat. He also texted Daeg and asked him to bring his truck out here. The SEALs had taught him it was always wise to establish an escape route early on.

Daeg was on it, too. Sure thing. Do I need to alert the cops now?

Right. Cal texted back: Ha ha.

Then, because Piper was taking her own sweet time getting back to him, he sent a couple of texts about the rescue dive program he'd put together.

"Make yourself at home, why don't you?"

Piper slouched in the doorway. She'd made one margarita. Apparently, he didn't merit a drink. Just sex. He patted the bed beside him.

"You coming over here?"

She glared, but she also looked tempted. He hadn't expected that. She took an angry swallow of her drink, and he had no idea what was running through her head. It must have been good, though, because her cheeks turned pink.

"You owe me a night." She took another drink.

"If you want." To his surprise, he meant it. What had started out as a joke and a dare was…something more?

She came over to the bed and he fought the urge to reach up and pull her down into his arms. She hadn't turned and run down the hallway, which was something, but he didn't know how far she really wanted this to go. So he took the margarita glass from her and took a drink. And shuddered. Piper didn't make margaritas any better than she compromised. The drink was sickly sweet, the tequila a distant afterthought. At least he'd be fine to drive.

She snatched the glass back from him, eyeing the drink level. Which was too bad. She should have brought enough to share.

"I should put tonight to good use." The smile lighting up her face was pure mischief. "How do you feel about bondage?"

Bondage wasn't something he'd ever been interested in experiencing firsthand. "If you tie me up, I'll tie you up."

Her eyes darkened and he sucked in a breath. She was thinking about it—and she was turned on.

"Piper," he crooned. He plucked the glass out of her hand and set it on the bedside table.

"I don't like you." She leaned forward.

The feeling was mutual. She was impetuous with an unforgivable side of rude. Plus, she'd insist on being in charge of any relationship she had, and he'd never let anyone—male or female—dominate him, in bed or out.

"Got it." When he leaned forward to meet her halfway, their foreheads touched and he caught a whiff of salt and tequila and something else. Something all Piper.

"You owe me," she whispered, like she was trying to convince herself.

"A bet's a bet," he agreed. Besides, if she got tonight, then he'd get another night. His pulse picked up as he thought about the possibility.

"So we'll just get each other out of our systems," she said, nodding like they'd both agreed to something.

"Piper?" He whispered her name against her mouth.

"Yeah?" Her tongue darted out to lick his bottom lip.

"Shut up."

He kissed her because he suddenly needed to, and he had no idea why. He'd never planned on kissing Piper, but her eyes said she might be thinking the same things he was, and heat shot through him at just the possibility. Her fingers curled in his T-shirt, tugging him closer, so he slid his hands along her neck, threading his fingers through her flyaway curls to hold her nearer still. He kissed her and she kissed him back, her mouth softening. Opening up to let him inside. Her breath came in little catches and he was pretty sure the rough groan he heard was his own. His brain had her name on a desperate soundtrack of *Piper Piper Piper*.

Her fingers discovered the hem of his shirt and tugged. Perfectly willing to help her out, he broke off their kiss long enough to help her draw his T-shirt over his head. She tossed it somewhere, wriggling out of her own shorts, and then ran her hands up his chest and over his shoulders. *Perfect*. He found her mouth again or she found his. He wasn't sure which, but it didn't matter. They were kissing each other again, long, slow, hot kisses. Her tongue swept into his mouth, taking charge, and he wanted to grin. And thump his chest. Roar out his pleasure. Any or all of the above.

Instead, he slid a thumb beneath the strap of her tank top, nudging the narrow strip down her shoulder. Taking the hint, she shimmied her arms out. He had to open his eyes. Her bra had teased him the whole way here, and, yeah…Piper had fabulous taste in lingerie. The satin cups were edged with something lacy and perfectly, wonderfully naughty.

"You're beautiful," he said hoarsely.

"More kissing," she demanded, uninterested in his opinions.

Kissing he could do. He swept his hands up and cupped her breasts through the soft fabric, rubbing a thumb over the plump curves as he gave her what she'd asked for. More kissing, more touching.

The familiar sound of trucks pulling into the driveway had him breaking off. *Shit.* Daeg might as well have marched a mariachi band down the driveway. Cal pulled back with a groan, resting his forehead against hers.

"This is why locking the door is a good thing."

The hard rap on her front door was followed by a brief pause. Cal could practically hear Daeg running the pros and cons of opening it. In a community as neighborly and tightly knit as this one, that was what you did. You knocked—and then you came in.

"You called in the cavalry?" Piper sat back. Her hair was drying into wayward corkscrews. Margarita making had apparently trumped finding a hairbrush. She looked sexy and mussed and the *last* thing he wanted to hear was Daeg's repeat knock.

He sat up and her hands fell away. "I figured you'd want me gone at some point, and I didn't want to walk."

Right. Because they both knew it wasn't outside the realm of possibility she might kick him out and make him hike the five miles back to town. In the dark.

"Would I do that to you?"

He looked at her. "I'm not sure. But we haven't always gotten along."

"Because you were bossy."

"You were reckless."

She made a show of looking down at her exposed bra. Daeg pounded again and called something. "Case in point?"

"Maybe."

She crossed her arms over her chest and settled back. "As long as we're clear."

He didn't know if her words were his cue to leave or not, but he swung his legs over the side of the bed and went to collect his keys.

PIPER'S WEEK HAD, frankly, sucked. Del planned on selling the dive shop out from under her. She hadn't gotten the Fiesta contract. Yet. She hadn't gotten the contract *yet*. Nothing was going the way she'd planned and, really, that had been the case since the man who'd been lying on her bed had pulled her out of the water five years ago.

The murmur of voices reached her from the front door. Then the door shut. She'd bet ten bucks Cal had locked it. Outside, a truck started up and drove off. She heard just the one engine, though, and wondered if Cal had decided to stay. Sure enough, he reappeared in the door of her bedroom.

"Daeg and Tag say hi," he said.

She flopped back onto the bed. "This is all your fault."

"Everything?" he asked, coming over.

Yes. No. She wasn't angry, more…at sea. She always had a plan and it always was a good one. Her plans worked out. Cal wasn't part of the plan. "You bet."

He leaned against the door frame and opened his arms wide. "You're in charge. I'm at your beck and call."

His small, lopsided grin had her wondering if he'd read her mind. That could be useful—or embarrassing.

Those three words—you're in charge—were the magic words she'd been waiting for, however. For no good reason, she wanted this man. She swung her legs over the side of the bed. Time to take action. Her hair was salty and tangled from a day in and on the water. She liked the way her hair curled after a dive, but she also had salt on her skin and in places she very much hoped Cal would be touching. *Kissing.*

He straightened up. "Are you leaving?"

One point for her.

"I want a shower." She paused just long enough to motion toward her margarita and then headed for the bathroom door, shooting him a naughty grin. He definitely brought out her inner bad girl. "Bring my drink."

"Is that an order?" His rough question had her pulse speeding up.

She smiled.

"Absolutely, beck-and-call boy."

She stepped into the bathroom, achingly aware of the man following her. She might have only one night—*two more,* her libido reminded her, but only one where she definitely got to be in charge—so she'd make every minute count. Her bathroom was the first room she'd remodeled in the cottage, because she loved baths. She'd scoured antiques shows in Marin County until she'd found the perfect piece, bribing one of her brothers to drag the heavy white claw-foot tub back to Discovery Island. It was big enough for two, but she'd also installed a rain shower.

She'd put every spare dime and hour she had into this room because it was her happy place, her refuge. From the slate tiles in soothing gray to the tub by the window, looking out over the beach, she'd built out her fantasies. Part of her wondered what Cal would think.

Part of her didn't care.

He was *hers.*

Temporarily, fantastically all *hers.*

She reached into the shower and hit the water before grabbing a stack of towels from the shelf. Rose-colored towels.

Pink.

"Pink? Really?"

She flashed him a grin. "Be glad I don't make you pose for a photo."

She turned and leaned against the sink. The white pedestal was a Victorian antique she'd scored for a song and refinished, the china cool and slick beneath her fingertips. How far would he let her push him?

He closed the door. Wow. She'd been close to Cal before—he'd ridden behind her on the way to her place—but this was different. This time, they both knew they were going to get naked and act out their secret fantasies. She'd known Cal for years, but the heat blasting through her was as unfamiliar as it was luscious.

"Strip," she said.

"Now I'm definitely hearing an order." His voice sounded rough and husky.

"Make it good," she suggested.

He didn't hold back any, either. "Tell me exactly what you want."

His eyes met hers, waiting for her to take charge.

No problem. She traced a finger down his thigh, feeling the hard muscle there. "Take it all off."

"You want to help?"

She thought about his question for a moment.

When she hesitated—*too many choices*—he made the decision for her. His fingers grasped the hem of his T-shirt and slowly pulled the cotton up, revealing the chiseled lines of his abdomen.

"Closer," she ordered throatily. She could look *and* touch. Not a problem.

He stepped toward her, until his feet brushed hers, and then sucked in a breath when she ran her fingers over the exposed skin.

"Perfect," she said as he yanked the shirt over his head and dropped it on the floor.

Then he *paused*. "Should I stop? Or call you mistress?"

The thick ridge beneath the buttons of his jeans was promising, too, and also all hers for tonight.

"Not unless you have a death wish." Sometimes, a woman had to be honest.

"Piper." Her name was half groan, half curse. She thanked the powers above that she got to him the way he got to her. "I'm pretty sure you're driving me crazy."

"I always do." She traced the waistband of his jeans and, *hello,* someone was definitely happy to see her. Cal bumped against her hand. She reached for the first button and popped it free.

"True."

"I'm just planning on doing it a little differently to-night."

"Piper." There was her name again. She wiggled her fingers, just a little, more because he felt good and she couldn't help but be aware of him beneath her palm. "We don't have to do this. The bet was a joke, not a legally binding contract."

"Are you saying you don't want to have sex with me?"

He braced his arms on either side of her on the sink, somehow managing to make her feel both secure and looked after. Those were new sensations for her, because she always took care of herself. Cal, on the other hand, looked after everyone. He made sure his friends and family—hell, the whole island—were safe and had what they needed. Apparently, he'd decided to include her in that number. She didn't want pity sex but something else entirely. And, she'd admit it, she hadn't misplaced her competitive spirit like she intended on misplacing her clothes.

If she was having sex with Cal, she was going to be the best he'd ever had.

"That's not what I'm saying at all," he said, but his voice

sounded husky. *Sexy,* and the tug she felt was something else unexpected. Since when had she found Cal attractive?

Since always, the little voice in her head chimed in.

"So, you do want me?" She moved her fingers and discovered she could stroke the very tip of him. She slid her fingertips in a small circle, and he sucked in a breath. The tiny inhalation was a definite yes, right there.

"We don't like each other." He sounded a little desperate, so she popped a second button, giving herself more room to work with. More Cal.

"Nope. We drive each other crazy." He was dead right.

It also wasn't fair how gorgeous he was. To compensate, she unbuttoned his third button.

"But we did have a bet," she said. "And I've never known you to renege on a bet."

"I'm a man of my word." A smile tugged at the corner of his mouth, and she'd never been so grateful for a bet before. This wasn't about winning or losing but about a chance to explore Cal. She had him for one wicked night—and then, because fair was fair and they'd both won or they'd both lost, depending on how you looked at it—she'd be *his*.

She could hardly wait.

"Off," she ordered and he gave her what she wanted.

He slid a finger beneath the last button on his jeans—there was nothing sexier than a man in button-up jeans, where she could slide the tips of her fingers between the gaps, stroke him where he was hot and hard—until it gave. Cal was commando. And lip-lickingly gorgeous.

His dark eyes watched her, but she discovered, his control was an illusion. When she touched him, he made a rough sound of pleasure, which only encouraged her to do it again. And again. She loved the way the groan slipped out. She wrapped a palm around him, literally holding Cal in the palm of her hand. He might not like her, but he definitely wanted her, and she could work with desire. He wasn't moving fast enough, though, so she tapped his hip, the little smack loud in the room. "Pick up the pace, Brennan."

He grinned at her as he shoved his jeans down his legs, and his crooked half smile went all the way to his eyes. This close to him, she could make out the faintest shadow of stubble on his jaw. Huh. Maybe Cal had a bad boy in him, after all. Or she'd been too busy pushing his buttons to take a really good look. *Or undoing his buttons.*

"I'm all yours. Do your best," he said.

His rough gasps and muttered curses were a power rush but also something more. She wasn't thinking about the something more tonight, so she pushed those thoughts away. Instead, she scraped the nails of her free hand lightly over his stomach, enjoying the way the muscles there— and Cal had more than his fair share of muscles—jumped. He liked this, too. A lot.

With her other hand, she stroked the length of him as she cupped him. He groaned, something incoherent, half prayer and half her name. Lucky him—she'd barely gotten started. She leaned forward.

PIPER WAS A take-charge woman. Cal had discovered that indisputable fact when he was ten and nothing had changed in the twenty years since. What had changed was how much he liked it. Liked *her.*

Her mouth surrounded him, hot wet perfection that made parts of him howl with pleasure. The strangest thing, though, was that this was *Piper.* While he was no angel, he usually insisted on having some kind of relationship with a woman before they went to bed together. He hadn't been holding out for a ring and happily ever after, but he hadn't been into the casual hookup and bar scene, either. Nor did

he think Piper was. Island gossip being what it was, he'd
have heard if she'd made a practice of casual hookups.

Piper's bathroom was getting dark, and he wished he'd
thought to flip on a light when he'd made the return trip
from her front door. He wanted to see her face as she made
love to him. Had sex with him. Or maybe both, if he was
lucky. He didn't know what this was, but the way she
made him feel was out-of-this-world good and like nothing he'd felt before.

Her mouth covered him, sinking down. His hips rose
up to meet her, and he was putty in her hands. He could
imagine the wicked gleam in her eyes if she knew. Which
she had to, because he was making all sorts of noises. He
skimmed his hands over her shoulders, her throat, tangling
his fingers in her curls. At some point, she'd lost her tie
and her hair was spread all over him. Another thing he
liked too much.

"Come up here so I can kiss you." The growly demand
was back in his voice.

"You lost a bet, Cal." Her fingers did something positively wicked to him at the same time. "Tonight's mine
and I'm in charge."

She lifted her mouth off him just enough to get the
words out. Each word was a hot whisper over his skin.
Nope. He wouldn't be lasting long tonight, and his immi-
nent loss of control was only partly due (very, very partly
due) to the fact he hadn't had sex in months.

Losing, however, didn't seem like such a bad thing when
she put it that way.

Just to prove his point, she licked her way up the length
of him.

"Please?" The word sounded needier than he liked, but
it worked.

Piper paused. Her fingers squeezed him deliciously,

briefly, and then she slid up his body. Her parts fit against his as she leaned in to kiss him.

His own hands got busy, stripping off her shirt and cupping her breasts, skimming the curves until he found the clasp in front. One quick flick, and she was shrugging out of the bra he'd admired so much. Her lingerie was still pretty, he decided—it was just that she was so much prettier. His eyes were getting used to the dark. Piper was all soft shadows and dark curves, but his imagination hadn't done her justice or considered the possibility of her intriguing tan lines and the paler places where her bikini had covered her up. Barely.

Right now, though, he was focused on baring her.

She liked what he was doing, too. She stilled for a moment before melting into his touch. The fierce relief sweeping through him was almost as shocking as the fact that they were here. Getting naked *together*. He didn't think Piper would go this far just to prove a point, but he'd never known with Piper. She was a leap-first, think-later kind of gal. Tonight, though, she was warm and willing, arching into his touch with a rough noise of pleasure. He wondered if he could make her scream. Or beg. Either one worked for him. Maybe both, if he were a very lucky man.

She kissed him harder and more fiercely, moving their kiss into new territory. This was no gentle meeting of their mouths but more like she'd decided to devour him, her tongue sweeping inside his mouth and taking what she wanted. He gladly opened for her.

He ran his hand down her back, tracing the straight arrow of her spine until he was cupping her butt through the silk of her panties. Since she wasn't letting go of his mouth, he wasn't asking for permission. Fair was fair.

Her thighs held his hips in a vise, and her mouth grew more frantic as she kissed him. He wanted to kiss her for hours, and yet at the same time, he wanted all of her right now. He pressed up into her sweet heat and about lost his mind. Since he wanted her lost with him, he moved his hand lower, curving his fingers inward to stroke her through her panties.

"IF YOU LIKE these panties, take them off." Cal's growly voice in her ear stoked the heat building inside Piper higher. Her SEAL definitely meant business, and his demand only worked her up more. She'd never been one for orders, but this was one command she could work with.

Not waiting for an answer, he hooked his thumbs in the sides of her panties and tugged. *Okay, then.*

She obligingly shimmied out of them—they *were* her favorites, after all, and there was no point in sacrificing them to hot sex if she could save them—and the scrap disappeared somewhere in the direction of her bedroom, leaving her naked in front of Cal. She wasn't so sure she was in charge anymore, but…it was okay. Scratch that. More than okay—more like downright fantastic.

"Shower time," he said roughly.

Right. *Shower.*

"I don't care." She didn't care anymore about concealing the truth. All she wanted was Cal and her bed, the two sounding like the perfect combination.

"Shh." His mouth brushed hers and then he scooped her up with one arm and headed for the shower, which was fortunately more than big enough for two. The hot water had steamed up the bathroom, blurring the edges. He set her on her feet on the water-warmed tiles and then stepped in, six-plus feet of hot, wet male she couldn't wait to hold. Even in the semidarkness, he was gorgeous, and when he held out a hand, it seemed natural to take it. His fingers curled around hers, pulling her into the stream of hot water. Nothing had prepared her for the heat, for the need burning through her.

She should have lit candles or had one of those aroma-therapy-dispenser things puffing sweet stuff out into the air. Cal didn't seem to mind the lack in the romance department. He pulled her in close, her thighs brushing his, her breasts pressed against his chest. *Heaven.*

There was enough steam in the room to make things fuzzy, like the best kind of dream. Plus, this close, she felt every inch of him, including the inches she'd just enjoyed. Cal held on to her until there was no missing how much he was relishing this shower of theirs.

And she'd barely gotten started.

She reached for him, but he spun her gently around and placed her hands on the tiled wall.

"You touch me now, and this shower's going to be over before it gets started," he growled.

"You have a problem with that?" Suddenly, soap and hot water didn't sound anywhere near as good as having her way with Cal and the impressive erection he was sporting. She slipped a hand behind her, reaching for him again.

He grunted, half amused, half impatient, then reached around her for the shampoo. "Behave."

"Overrated," she said, palming him.

"Good thing I don't mind misbehaving with you some." His rough whisper echoed in her ear. Then his big fingers were massaging the shampoo through her hair. He was *good.* Or bad. She gave up trying to figure it out, just let herself sink into the sensual press of his fingers against her head as he worked the lather for long, dreamy minutes. She had no idea a shampoo could be so sensual. His nails scratched erotically across her scalp, sending small shivers down her spine.

He didn't stop there, either. When her hair was clean,

he started in with the washcloth. The soft rain fell around them, comforting and soothing, until she was all but bone-less. The cloth traveled over her shoulders, down her arms. He bathed her with the same thoroughness with which he approached everything. Her back and her butt. Her front.

Oh, yes, please.

He ran the soapy cloth down her breasts. Once. Then again when she pushed her breasts into his hand in silent demand. Her nipples were deliciously sensitive, tighten-ing into greedy nubs as he traced a wicked circle around the straining tips.

Needing more, she arched back into him. "Cal—"

"You bet," he answered roughly.

"Let's—" She didn't finish her sentence or even her thought. The cloth dipped lower, moving down past her stomach to her core.

"Let's let me take care of you, okay?" His ragged breathing promised he was right there with her, and let-ting Cal have his way didn't seem like a bad idea at all.

"Right now," she demanded.

And he did.

He touched her intimately with the cloth, nothing but four-hundred-count Egyptian cotton between his fingers and her flesh. The rough friction of the material was even better than bare skin, letting her prolong the sweet, steady ache. She was close, her body tightening, bearing down on him.

"Tease," she muttered.

"I'm not teasing."

When, long minutes later, he reached to turn off the water, she scrambled to get out first because there was something too devastatingly sensual about Cal looking after her. The truth was he overwhelmed her. Fantastically, wonderfully so, but she was losing control of her body in a way she never did. She wrapped a rose-colored—*pink*—towel around her and padded into the bedroom, leaving him to follow her.

PIPER WAS STILL determined to be in charge, to be the one giving the orders. Sexy, yes. Cal loved the way she knew what she liked and how her sensuality didn't embarrass her. Piper was as all out in bed as she was diving. Or living. Piper didn't hold back. But he wanted something more from her.

He wanted her to trust him.

He followed her into the bedroom, turning different options over in his head.

"Do you trust me?" This night was for her, but for some things, he wanted permission.

She had to think about her answer, which wasn't the response he'd been hoping for. "Piper—"

He knew she didn't want a discussion or a conversation. She wanted hot, meaningless sex. With him, though, which apparently meant what they did in her bed wasn't going to be meaningless. Not for him.

Her knees hit the edge of the mattress. "Yes."

"Yes, you trust me?"

"You want a notarized document?" she growled back. "Because I can absolutely get up and get one for you, right now."

He couldn't stop the smile from flashing across his face. "Remember, you offered."

She'd been warned.

CAL TURNED AWAY from the bed and if he wasn't looking for a condom, she'd kill him.

"Top drawer," she said. "On the left-hand side. There are condoms."

He made a rough sound, half protest, half amused. So, yeah, she liked being in charge. She knew what she liked, too. He'd have to deal with it.

He came back, though, setting a foil packet by the side of the bed. That wasn't all he had. He also had a handful of her sarongs. The thin strips of mesh fabric tied over her hips and hinted at the bikini bottom beneath. She had no idea what kind of fashion statement he intended to make.

"Modest much?"

He gave her a look she couldn't quite interpret.

"I'm going to tie you up."

A statement of intent, her brain noted through the lightning bolt of heat torching her body. Not a question at all.

"Any questions?" he asked roughly. "Objections?"

She should object. She really, really should but…he'd made her think about it. About how it would feel to be at Cal's sensual mercy, her body his to touch. Instead of protesting, she shook her head.

"Good."

He made quick work of tying her up, carefully fastening her wrists to the headboard. Just her wrists, and not so tight she couldn't get free if she needed to, but tight enough to remind her she wasn't going anywhere easily.

"Now you're all mine." The look in his eyes got her going. She'd wanted to take him, to take advantage of being the one in charge, but he'd turned the tables on her…and she loved it. Arousal shot through her. She'd never been the kind of woman who needed or wanted a man to take charge, but this was…wicked sexy.

He ran a finger over her stomach and the muscles there fluttered nervously, as though she had a thousand highly aroused and nervous butterflies flapping around in there. Being tied up, even as a game, made her feel vulnerable. Which was something she didn't do. Of course, Cal didn't like opening up, either, which made them a good match on some levels. Now, however, she couldn't *do* anything but wait. And anticipate, her brain on overload suggesting possible fantasies.

Too late, she thought of a question. "Do I get to tie *you* up on your night?"

One night was definitely *not* going to be enough.

"I should gag you," he said tenderly, brushing his fingers over her mouth. "You look beautiful."

Heat curled through her as he touched her intimately. *Perfect.*

"Kiss me some more," she demanded as his fingers did something positively wicked and she clenched deep inside. His hand urged her leg up around his hip, another good idea she decided with a breathy moan.

Like always, he didn't hesitate. He decided—and then he did. "Absolutely."

Like her words were some kind of permission he'd been waiting for, he took charge, lifting her effortlessly as he moved down the bed. She squeaked. To her eternal mortification, she made an inelegant, embarrassed sound of surprise.

"Cal—"

"Shh. My turn." She felt his rough whisper against her core. Her very bare, very exposed core. He kissed her and then she completely lost it. He had her whimpering and groaning, and there might have been begging involved, although she'd deny it if asked. His big hands on her hips kept her right where he wanted her, his fingers dipping in to tease and part her. And his mouth...she lit up like a forest fire from the heat and pleasure.

"Cal—" She squeaked his name out, and her reward was a very male sound of appreciation. He kissed her some more, clearly in no rush, as deliberate and thorough about this as he was about everything. If she'd known he was this good, she'd have jumped him sooner, she thought, dazed.

"Now it's your turn," he said against her, and the hot whisper of his words right there, where she was tight and slick, sent her over the edge in a rush. She came shockingly fast, rocking against him.

There was a rustle as he untied her and conjured up the condom. *Yes*.

"May I?" he asked, and there was no holding back the smile splitting her face.

"My pleasure," she said, wrapping her legs around his waist. He'd won the first round, but... She grinned and pushed, until he rolled over so she straddled him. Threading her fingers through his, she pinned his hands over his head. "You cheated."

"You're complaining?" She gripped his hips with her knees and sank slowly down.

"Absolutely not." He groaned out the words.

She loved his body, she decided. He was all hard, tempting muscles and ridges in all sorts of delicious places. She couldn't wait to explore him, so she sank down a little farther.

"Just making my point." She leaned forward and nipped his ear.

The touch was his tipping point, because he bit out a curse and surged upward. "Piper—"

There. She wriggled and took the last inch of him. "*Now* it's my turn."

She began to move and, nope, he didn't have any complaints. Even when it was her turn for a very, very long time.

10

A MALE ARM pinned her to the bed. An arm that matched the leg tossed casually over her own leg. Piper squinted and spotted her panties on the floor in the dim morning light. Getting dressed seemed like a logical next step, so she worked her way out from beneath the arm and sat up. She preferred sleeping with the curtains open because she liked seeing the ocean. Plus, it wasn't as if she had neighbors. Other than the very occasional fisherman or motorboat, there was no one to see in. Liberated, she stood up and padded over to the window. Yep. Same ocean view she'd admired every morning for the past two years. The difference lay in the bed behind her. Resting her forehead against the glass, she postponed turning around.

The rustle of sheets warned her time was up. "Piper?"

Cal's raspy voice made her melt and sent heat shooting through her body. Apparently, one night hadn't been enough to get him out of her system, after all.

"Present and accounted for," she said, when what she really wanted to say was "How come you're still here?" It would have been easier if he'd done the walk of shame to his truck and gone home. Maybe. Or maybe he wasn't a morning person and it was still too early for him to be thinking. She didn't know. They'd skipped all the dating preliminaries and gone straight for the good stuff.

"Are you coming back to bed?" Did he want her to? She was a morning person.

"I'm up." She padded barefoot over to the door. Maybe other people managed their mornings-after more smoothly, but talking just seemed awkward. Cal sat up, the sheet falling to his waist, and she revised her opinion. Naked was a good look for Cal.

"Is there something I'm supposed to say here?" He ran a hand over his head.

"I'm making coffee." It had to be the lack of caffeine that had her considering crawling back into bed with him. "I've got work to do. Contracts to win. You can have the first shower."

"Right." He swung his legs over the side of the bed. *Do* not *look,* she told herself as he swiped his clothes off the floor.

She kept repeating those words to herself over the course of the next twenty minutes while she made coffee and scared up a muffin. She was still trying to convince herself she'd succeeded when she parked her butt in a chair down by the water and finally admitted she'd failed.

Have sex with Cal.

Get him out of her system.

Hah.

Her plan was an epic backfire. She'd had sex with him. *Once.* And, hallelujah, it was likely going to happen a second time—she owed him a night, after all, and Cal always collected on their bets.

He'd taken charge of her, of her body. And she'd *liked* it.

Correction.

She'd loved it.

Out here, alone with her thoughts and the ocean, she

could be honest with herself. She'd had no idea that *not* fighting with Cal could be so much fun. Toe-curling, senses-devastating fun. Apparently, he had hidden depths. She should have been plotting her dive program and figuring out how best to wow the Fiesta team. Instead…she was wondering if her night with Cal also included the morning after. And making a mental note to negotiate future bets more carefully.

Cal wasn't just the Grim Reaper raining disapproval on her actions. He was *sweet. Thoughtful.* And he had a sense of humor. She'd known some of those things before—after all, anyone who came up with a bet where the loser wore a red, white and blue string bikini clearly had a fine sense of the ridiculous (and he'd agreed to wear the suit if he'd lost, so he was also fair). He'd also carted her butt down the sunbaked dock yesterday, like some kind of Sir Lancelot. At least, she thought that was the guy who'd tossed his grade-A and probably ermine-lined cloak over a mud puddle so his queen could keep her feet dry. Or maybe that was Sir Raleigh. Whoever the guy was, Cal had made her feel special last night.

Special.

Like there was nothing he wouldn't do for her.

Funny how she'd felt something suspiciously similar when he'd jackknifed into the water at Rose Wall. She wasn't stupid and he'd never been a good liar. Something had gone wrong, and it hadn't been with his equipment.

Equally clear, he didn't want to talk about it. Keeping silent might be just a guy thing. A fish or a piece of seaweed had brushed his leg, and he'd startled. He was embarrassed. The big, tough navy SEAL had overreacted and was covering.

But…she didn't think so.

SEAL training wasn't some kind of covert op. While

she'd never trained herself to be a SEAL or a rescue swimmer, she'd heard stories. Watched the videos on YouTube. Any man who could swim three hundred and fifty feet underwater before surfacing for a breath of air? That man wouldn't have been worried by a leaky snorkel.

Nope. She suspected it was something else.

There had been plenty of island gossip about Cal's last mission. Things had gone wrong, and his team had lost a man, or so she'd heard. He'd come home, but maybe he'd brought some mental baggage with him. Or he'd been injured and hadn't wanted to tell anyone—again, just like Cal. She looked back toward the house. She could ask him.

In fact, she'd tried.

He'd shot her down. Deflected her with a night of hot sex.

The decoy routine alone was almost reason enough to ask him again before she started jumping to conclusions.

Or was tempted to read anything else into their night. Hot sex did not a relationship make, and she couldn't afford to forget, not with the Fiesta contract on the line.

CAL DIDN'T GIVE up control—ever—and he'd certainly never played bondage games. Or any kind of games. Piper challenged those rules, just like she challenged everything else. Her wicked bet had him out of control. And the problem wasn't just the sexual chemistry that made it hard to focus on anything but luring Piper back to bed—it was their fundamentally different approaches to diving. To life. To everything.

He did plenty of thinking while he showered, per Her Highness's royal command. He wasn't stupid enough to refuse the offer. These old cabins had notoriously flaky water heaters and he preferred hot water. Piper might have returned to the island two years ago—thank you island gossip—but she'd clearly been doing some redecorating since her arrival. The small bathroom had a new ceramic-tile floor and a sea-foam-green coat of paint. Her selection of shampoos and soaps were correspondingly girlie, and he either tolerated smelling like a fruit bowl when he got done or went dirty.

Using her shampoo caused trouble in the wanting-Piper department. She'd specified one night but, as he squirted apple-scented shampoo into his hand and lathered up, parts of him wanted to abandon the shower and go after her. Maybe she'd have downed enough coffee to shake the grumpiness and make her amenable to going back to bed. He didn't know what she wanted. Hell. He didn't know what *he* wanted, just that the Fiesta Cruise Lines folks had put both of them in an untenable position and he didn't see any way out of it.

She wanted to provide resort dives to new divers, while he wanted to focus on technically challenging dives. His business plan would offer dives for the select and the best of the best—while she believed everyone should have a chance to slip underwater and *see*. This wasn't kindergarten. Not everyone left with a gold sticker and a trophy, but convincing Piper would take a miracle. She was one of the most stubborn people he'd ever met.

Of course, her willfulness also extended to bed, and he had no complaints about *that* at all. He was just starting to heat back up again remembering last night when the water temperature proved the plumbing hadn't improved with time. The pipes groaned, wheezed and then drenched him in icy water. The unexpected cold shower took care of his erection, so he got out and toweled off, dropping his used towel into the empty linen basket. After pulling his clothes back on, he moved out in search of Piper, who'd clearly bolted with no intention of returning. She wasn't in the bedroom or the kitchen, although both rooms bore clear signs of her passing, since Piper wasn't a tidy person.

She'd accomplished her mission in the kitchen. The room smelled of coffee beans and fresh brew, although there was no Piper. He poured himself a cup from her Mr. Coffee and cleaned up the damage. There was sugar on the counter, along with an open carton of half-and-half, a partially eaten muffin, which couldn't possibly sustain life, and a dirty spoon. It wasn't hard to figure out where she'd gone. Not only was the porch door open, but she'd left a little trail of disaster behind her, including an abandoned newspaper, muffin crumbs and the coffee cup sitting on an end table by the windows. Since the cup was still warm and therefore presumably fresh carnage, he snagged it, because she clearly was the kind of woman who, morning person or not, needed her caffeine in order to be civilized. He wasn't going to push his luck.

When he stepped outside, she was parked in an Adirondack chair down on the scrap of beach. Little waves teased her flip-flops, but she didn't seem to mind that her toes were definitely getting wet or that the ocean had attained a balmy fifty-five degrees.

He nudged her shoulder with his hip and offered her the cup. She traded him a smile for the mug, so he was already in the black for the day. He wasn't sure what he'd expected after her sudden flight from the bed.

"So," she said, taking a slurp from her mug, which had him wincing. "What's your plan for the day?"

Asking, not telling. On the other hand, she'd said "your" and not "our," so clearly, he still had his work cut out for him.

"Because I thought we should discuss next steps on the diving proposal," she said, as if they were purely business acquaintants and last night had never happened.

It was all very civilized. He half expected her to whip out a planner and start penciling him in. She obviously wasn't fighting the same urges he was. To reach out and put his mouth on her neck. To run his fingers down her arm and tug her back into bed with him. Nope. She was all business.

"We need to finalize our sites," she said. "We should probably coordinate our diving partners, as well, decide which boat we're going to take—that kind of stuff."

Going back to bed was apparently off the table. Good to know. "Your plan sounds fine," he said gruffly.

"Okay, good. We'll reconvene on Monday." She gave him a tentative smile.

Monday was two days—and nights—from now.

"Come with me now." He blurted the words out without thinking. "You know my mother. She does Saturday-morning brunch and there's always room for one more."

"Why?" Piper asked.

He ran a hand over his head. "Because you need to eat? And my mother cooks enough food for a small army?"

He had a place of his own just down the road from his mother, but he usually ate at her house. It was a win-win situation. He kept an eye on his mother; she fed him. He hadn't been home long enough to worry about dating. It wasn't like he had time, plus he wasn't exactly relationship worthy at the moment. Of course, Piper had made it perfectly clear she was using him only for his body. He knew he was grinning but he'd just had the best sex of his life last night and he was in a good mood. He wasn't letting Piper ruin that.

She didn't look precisely overwhelmed by his breakfast offer, however. "Last night doesn't change anything. We're not dating."

"Did I ask you out on a date?" Piper and him on a date? The thought wasn't all that bad.

She slurped at her coffee. "Nope. I wasn't sure if the omission was an oversight on your part or not."

Holding back his laugh was impossible. That was Piper. Supremely confident. "You were the one who took advantage of me. I think any dating moves should come from you."

She eyed the bottom of her mug. "How is this my fault?"

"You told me to get on your bike. And then you had your way with me." He squatted next to her, hands cupping his own mug when what he really wanted was to be touching her. Huh. Imagine that.

"That's one interpretation."

"So I'm hearing a no for breakfast?"

He had to get going. He had a hundred things to do today, and there was no way his mother hadn't noticed his absence last night. She might not say anything—although there was a fifty-fifty chance she would—but he'd swear she had her own secret spies or a highly developed Spidey sense, because she'd always noticed when one of his siblings had stayed out overnight. Saturday-morning breakfast was not optional. He'd thought… He didn't know what he'd thought. Pancakes and sausage weren't a diamond ring, and Piper had eaten breakfast at his house before. She had no business getting huffy with him. Plus, she had to be hungry.

Right on cue, her stomach growled, because as he'd suspected, half a muffin did not a breakfast make.

"I rest my case."

"I'm not coming with you." She'd done that more than once last night, which was apparently the problem.

"Why not?"

She stared at him for a moment. Maybe it was a girl

thing, but he had no idea what he'd said wrong. "I just had sex with my main competition for the Fiesta contract."

"You were amazing," he said and he meant it, too. Again, apparently not the right thing to say, because she sighed.

"You owe me quarters," she said pointedly. "Lots and lots of quarters."

"*I* make you swear?"

"You make me do a lot of things, but this one's all on me." She fiddled with her coffee cup. "We shouldn't have done this, but it's been a long time coming. We've had this chemistry thing between us for years, and I guess I shouldn't be surprised it kind of bubbled over last night."

He'd never heard really hot sex described out loud as a chemistry thing that bubbled over, but she could call their night whatever she wanted as long as he got to repeat it again.

"So no breakfast?"

"Having sex would be a conflict of interest."

"No breakfast. Got it."

HER COFFEE CUP wasn't going to magically replenish itself. Piper snuck a peek at Cal. She was probably pushing her luck to ask him for a refill. Or anything else. She still didn't know why he was sticking around or making offers of breakfast. Worse, part of her wanted to say yes and hop in his truck with him.

She'd had sex with him.

Super hot, fantastic, slightly kinky sex.

That, she could do. Brunch with Cal's mother? Not so much. They were childhood acquaintances, sure, and if the Brennans were hosting a two-hundred-person barbecue, she (and the rest of the island) would expect an invite. An intimate weekend brunch, however, was so far out of her league he might as well have invited her to Mars. Saturday morning was for family and she wasn't that.

She scooped a stone from the sand. So what if she wanted to go? They both watched her stone skip over the water. Once. Twice. And...sink. Yep. Pretty much like her heart.

"Not bad." He leaned down and snagged a stone. "Watch and learn."

The playful gleam in his eye had her thinking about going back to bed. Maybe they could *both* not go to brunch. *No.* Bad libido. She had to get this chemistry thing under control.

He launched the stone with a smooth flick of his wrist. The scruff on his jaw made him look impossibly sexy and more than a little rumpled. Apparently, he was not only a rock star in bed, but he was also king of skipping stones, because his stone sailed over the waves, ignoring her silent jinxes.

"One. Two. Three. *Four.*"

The stone sank beneath a wave. *Darn it.* He'd smoked her.

Which didn't mean she had to give in easily. Or even graciously. "The last one didn't count."

He raised a brow. "You're a sore loser."

Probably, but this was *Cal,* and she wasn't giving up yet. "Plus, mine went farther."

"If you want to swim out there and compare rocks, go right ahead."

"Pass."

His phone buzzed and he pulled it out of his back pocket. "I've got to go."

She'd known that since he woke up. Standing up, he brushed a kiss over her mouth.

Say something.

"I'll see you on Monday?"

She made her words half question, half polite brush-off. Monday was good. They'd already settled their work schedule. What was still undecided, however, was how they were going to deal with the chemistry they had between them.

"You still owe me a night."

"Oh." *Yes, please.*

"You can bet I'm collecting," he growled.

THE BRENNAN PLACE was a big, rambling home perched above the ocean. The house had a seemingly endless supply of bedrooms and hidey-holes, all of which had been a lifesaver growing up, as Cal's parents had been fairly prolific. He had three younger sisters and two brothers. His mother was the center of their universe, and he was more than okay with that. He was fortunate to have always had her at his back. She'd understood when he'd enlisted and left the island, but she'd also made it clear he'd always have a home. His father's unexpected death from a heart attack three years ago had been rough, but they'd weathered it together, because they were family, and family stuck.

He *had,* however, bought his own place just down the road, when he'd been home on leave, a fixer-upper, which he was slowly restoring on the weekends. He loved his family, but he didn't need to be glued at the hip with them. Since he'd moved back to the island permanently only six months ago, the cottage was still a work in progress. Or, as his sisters called it, a disaster with potential. In the plus column, he had two bedrooms, one bathroom and a Day-Glo-green kitchen, which opened up to a living room area with a panoramic view of the ocean. The minus column had been enough to lower the price to bargain territory, however. The roof leaked, the hot water was more temperamental than Tag without coffee, and Cal had pulled up the shag carpeting only to learn that the hardwood underneath must have been used by a small herd of dogs and boys to run the Indy 500 with cleats on. After a quick pit stop to change his clothes and run his eyes over the day's to-do list, he walked up the road to the family place. Two of his younger sisters were there, home from college for the summer. His third sister was in Paris, practicing her French. Or, at least, he hoped she was practicing her French and not meeting sexy French men. Luke, his baby brother, was home on leave from the U.S. Army Rangers. It promised to be a loud, boisterous, fun brunch.

They liked Piper. They liked her family. No one would have questioned her presence, although they might have wondered how he and Piper had arrived together without killing each other. Their spats were family legend, as were the paybacks and practical jokes.

His mother was in the kitchen when he arrived. After popping the requested juice into the fridge, he went up behind her, wrapped his arms around her waist and dropped a kiss on her cheek.

"You took your time getting here." She was smiling when she said it, so he wasn't in trouble yet.

"And yet I still have first dibs on the bacon." He reached around her to snag a crispy strip from the stack on the plate. She'd already fried at least two pounds of bacon, and there was a roll of paper towels conveniently close by to clean up the carnage. Those were the perfect ingredients for a Saturday morning. He thought about Piper going without bacon and decided it was her loss. He'd wanted her to come, but she'd turned him down.

He kind of wished she were here. Piper and bacon on a Saturday morning would be even better. His mother smacked his hand away from the plate but not before he'd snagged two more pieces. He took his prize and leaned against the counter.

"I'd make bacon for you on other mornings. It doesn't have to be a Saturday-morning exclusive," she grumbled.

"It tastes better on Saturdays?" Plus, he didn't need to kill himself. Too much of a good thing wouldn't help when he had to swim five hundred yards in twelve minutes. But this was bacon and exceptions had to be made.

She hummed her agreement and poured pancake batter onto her griddle. He crunched his way through the bacon, considered stealing a fourth piece, then washed his hands and moved next to her to chop potatoes. He knew the deal.

"How's work? Did you get your contract?"

The status of said contract was a popular question. "When we get the Fiesta contract, I'll be able to expand. I've got feelers out on adding a new location. It would be good to keep the command center separate from our gear, and I want to bring on some other guys getting out of the service."

She deftly flipped a pancake onto the growing stack. His siblings ate enough for an entire SEAL unit. "You're sure about landing the deal?"

He grinned. "It's down to us and Dream Big and Dive. We're going to win."

She poured a new batch of pancakes. "That's Piper Clark's place, right?"

"Yep." He slid the potatoes into a free pan. "She's running a place down on the boardwalk."

"How is Piper?"

He'd bet his mother had seen Piper at least once this week. The island simply wasn't that big, and he made a mental note to check his mother's Facebook page—and the ultimate source of island gossip—soon. If his mother had proof he and Piper were together (and while they weren't *together,* they weren't not together, either), she'd post the news for everyone to read.

"Piper's fine," he said carefully, not wanting to give the game away.

Better than fine. The memories of last night were the forever kind of memories. Piper in bed was spectacular. This morning had been pretty great, too, right up until the moment when she'd kicked him out. He'd liked sharing a cup of coffee with her. When they weren't fighting, she was great company.

"Uh-huh." His mother's snort of laughter said it all. "How many fights have the two of you had so far?"

He counted. Zero, zip and *nada.* No fights in the past twelve hours had to be a record. Apparently the one place he and Piper agreed was in bed.

"We're not so bad."

His mother eyed the bubbles forming in the center of the pancakes and teased up the edge of one with her spatula. "You're worse. The two of you are like oil and water. Whatever one does, the other takes issue with."

"She's stubborn. She always wants to do things her way."

"And you don't?"

"Aren't you supposed to take my side?"

"If you want unconditional love, get a dog."

"Isn't this where you segue into the speech about finding a girl and settling down?"

"Piper's still single."

Danger. "And you just pointed out that she never agrees with me about anything. A lack of consent is going to make the I-do part of the wedding ceremony difficult."

He had a quick mental image of Piper getting married. She wasn't a big, puffy gown kind of person—he still shuddered when he remembered his sister's dress—but he could see her barefoot on the sand in something simple and short. She'd look good. Not, of course, that he had any business imagining Piper getting married. Whoever the guy was who took her on, he'd probably take issue with last night's shenanigans. Plus, Cal wasn't ready to give her up yet.

"It doesn't have to be Piper, although she's a nice girl. Settling down is a good thing."

"And it comes with fringe benefits," announced a throaty female voice behind them. Allie always enjoyed teasing him about marriage, probably because she'd met her own match in college. If Cal ever had daughters, he was sending them to an all-girls school. In the middle of nowhere. She and Dan had gotten married last year up in Napa. Cal didn't know much about weddings, but the winery had been busting out all over in flowers and his sister had glowed. Plus, they'd thrown a reception in the wine cave, and while he was more of a beer guy, he'd discovered that the right Pinot Noir was a beautiful thing.

Allie patted the small bump in her middle. His sister hadn't wasted any time in procreating. "I'm winning this race."

"And I don't recall entering."

She shrugged. "You've never seen a race you didn't want to win."

True.

"She's right." His mother passed Allie the platter heaped with pancakes. It was possible the food outweighed her. It definitely outweighed the baby bean. "She's going to give me my first grandchild. You need to catch up."

"Nice try," he said and picked up the plate of bacon. The plate was going right by his own place at the table.

"I do what I can." His mother shrugged modestly. "But Allie's still winning."

Allie winked and headed for the dining room. "Which

means you're batting for the losing team," she called over her shoulder.

"You give the rest of the family this much of a hard time?"

His mother's grin said it all. He knew she loved him. Of course, she also wanted to love a few grandchildren, at least a half dozen, and he hoped to God that number covered the whole clan, because he didn't see himself having six kids. He knew his limits. Plus, his baby momma would probably collapse from the shock of raising so many Brennans. She'd need to have nerves like Piper's to take his family on.

"I've got high hopes for you," she said, and he snorted.

"Hope all you want, but I'm not producing a ring. I'd need to be dating first."

He didn't know what this thing between him and Piper was but…it wasn't dating.

His mother brushed past him as he held the door open with his shoulder. She paused and inhaled dramatically. "Apples. Very nice."

Busted.

USUALLY, PIPER ENJOYED Saturday afternoons. She went for a swim. She cleaned the house and picked out recipes for all the meals she wouldn't actually cook in the coming week. Today she was restless, though, so she extended her time in the water. Cal had gone off to his family brunch, and she'd hook up with him the day after tomorrow. For *work,* she reminded herself. They weren't dating or hooking up in any kind of romantic fashion. Discovery Island was a small place in more ways than one. Once the gossip paired them together, things would get sticky. The FBI had nothing on her neighbors when it came to ferreting out information.

Discovery Island might be in the Pacific Ocean, but it

was no Tahiti. The water never warmed up above sixty-eight degrees, and in another month, she'd be risking hypothermia if she so much as stuck a toe in without a wet suit on, but Piper had always loved swimming with the sea lions that gathered just off the island's northern coast. There might also be a small chance of running into a shark hunting for dinner, but she'd take that. Endearingly awkward on dry land, the sea lions were all sleek power as they drilled through the water.

"Give me a heads-up if you spot a shark, okay?"

She'd already borrowed her quota of trouble for the day.

The sea lion next to her barked, and she decided to take the noise as an affirmative.

The sun was out, lighting up the water and the kelp forests beneath her. She turned back after a half mile, mentally waving goodbye to her sea lion pals. They'd head over to a patch of rocks another mile away and then pull themselves out to sun the afternoon away. Sea lions definitely had the right ideas.

She somersaulted lazily in the water, traveling underwater until her air ran out and she burst to the surface. Her pace wasn't competitive, but it felt good. When she reached her beach and waded out, her muscles burned, tired in a good way.

Mission accomplished. She'd be able to button her jeans this week.

She padded back to the house, rinsing off her feet with the garden hose before going inside. Tracking sand everywhere when she was ten and didn't have to clean it up herself was one thing. Now she was in charge of the Hoover, she was more careful.

Her place was warm and cozy in the early-afternoon sunlight. She could feel a book and a nap beckoning.

And...she smelled bacon? She wouldn't have overlooked bacon, and she knew to an item the sad state of her pantry.

She followed her nose into the kitchen.

Someone had left a covered plate of food on her counter, clearly the source of the bacon goodness filling her house. When she popped off the tinfoil, she discovered bacon, muffins, crispy slices of ham and a slice of chocolate cake as out of place as it was welcome. *Oh, yeah.*

She read the note and smiled.

Lock your door, Piper....

Her navy rescue swimmer definitely had a soft side, after all.

11

PIPER HATED NOT pulling her weight. So since the mountain—the mountain here being Mount Brennan—didn't come to Piper on Monday, she went to the mountain. She barged through the door of Deep Dive, carrying a messenger bag stuffed to the gills with notes, dive-site descriptions and her laptop.

Tag was manning the counter. "He's in the command center," he said without looking up from his laptop.

Apparently word had gotten around about their partnership. Hopefully, that was all it was, because she'd decided the best way to handle her hookup with Cal was to pretend publicly that it hadn't happened. Business first, bedroom second. If she was looking forward to her next night with Cal, well, no one else on the island needed to know *that*.

She went around the counter, opened the door to the backroom and—holy moly—stepped into an entirely different world. She'd assumed "command center" was a male euphemism for "place where we keep all our toys" or "fancy name to make ourselves feel important." Nope. Cal really had built a command center. Floor-to-ceiling monitors displayed the latest weather information and all sorts of interesting dots and blips. A bank of computers and screens took up most of the floor space.

Cal and Daeg were bent over a screen at the far end.

"Are you planning to take over the world?" It actually appeared to be a viable option.

Daeg grinned. "Are you volunteering to assist?"

"It looks like you've got it covered." They stocked some serious hardware.

Cal straightened up and came over to her. She wasn't sure if she should stick out a hand, slap him on the back, like one of the guys, or French kiss him. He looked tired, though, so she decided to cut him some slack. Or going easy on him could have had something to do with how his big, suntanned body looked in a ragged T-shirt and another pair of white-at-the-seams blue jeans. He wore his usual steel-toed boots, as well, which was a look that definitely worked for her.

"What do you want, Piper?"

"Hello? Joint presentation and hands-on demo for Fiesta? I wanted to get started." *On Saturday.*

"Right." He stared at her, and she wondered if she had food on her face. Or magic marker. A second nose. Something, anything to explain the intensity of his gaze. "You want to work on our demo."

Why else would she be here?

"We have a week," she pointed out. "Seven days minus a few hours. We need to get going."

She dumped her bag on one of Cal's desks and fished out a list. "I've got a short list of dive sites to check out. My boat is gassed up and ready to go. So get your butt in gear, and we'll be out of here. Alternatively, feel free to drop out of the competition at any time, because I can handle it."

"I'll bet you can," he said drily.

She met his eyes and found humor and—wait for it—a

side of irritation. Too bad. He hadn't suggested a plan and she had. Since she appeared to be the only one with a viable one, they went with her idea.

"Maybe I'm busy right now."

"I'll survive," Daeg tossed out. "If you and Piper have a prior date."

They both turned and glared at him. Out of bed, this had to be the first time the two of them had ever been in sync on anything.

"The ideas are great," he said. "But you don't get to waltz in here and decide our plan of attack."

"I texted. You didn't respond."

"And you interpreted nonresponse as permission to do things your way?"

Well, yeah. The lines on either side of his nose got deeper, however, and she recognized that look as the one Cal got right before he told her precisely why he disliked her current course of action and everything that could go wrong.

And…bingo.

"Fiesta asked us to work together. That's not code for 'give me an ultimatum.'"

"You didn't respond. I took charge." She shrugged. "I don't have a problem with that."

"I do," he gritted out.

"Then, you should have answered my texts." She grabbed her bag and turned toward the door. "Move it."

She ignored the muttered curse behind her. He didn't have to like it—or her—as long as he got his butt in gear. He must have gotten the memo, because he fell in step with her.

"You're going to bc a pain in my butt, aren't you?" He opened the door for her and she breezed through. See? She could compromise.

"Probably," she agreed. "Or, you can do things my way."

"We did that Friday night." He snagged his keys from the counter. "Now it's my turn and I'm driving."

CAL PILOTED THE *Dive Boat I* out of the marina. Eventually he and Piper had compromised. He drove today and they used his boat. The next time they went, they'd use hers. Piper actually hadn't protested much, and Cal suspected the reason for that was the flawless weather. After they'd gotten going, she'd parked herself up front, soaking in the sunshine. She looked perfectly content, her sunglasses on and a slightly grubby ball cap pulled low over her forehead.

Just when he thought she might be taking a catnap, she looked over at him. "So. *Dive Boat I?*"

He concentrated on guiding the boat out of the marina. Discovery Island's mayor—the only person who had run for the underpaid job last election—had tied up his hundred-foot motor yacht in such a way that the expensive boat stuck out, making access to open water challenging. Either bad parking skills or a desire to make sure everyone knew he'd bought a new boat, Cal had no idea which. "You don't like the name?"

"It's not a name. It's a shortcut."

She leaned back on her elbows, making herself at home. The narrow straps of her bikini top peeked out from the edges of her T-shirt. She was wearing yet another pair of cutoff shorts and flip-flops. She'd toed off her shoes as soon as she climbed on board and pulled her hair back in a ponytail, errant curls blowing in the breeze. The other night, her hair had been spread out on her pillow, little strands tickling his nose and his face. He didn't want to be out here on the water with her. Nope. Where he really wanted to be was back in her bed. Or his. He'd slept with his share of beautiful women, but she was different.

She waved her list at him again. "We'll start with Pup Alley," she said, naming a popular dive site where sea lions and their pups were often spotted.

And not just because she was so stubborn.

"I'm driving the boat," he pointed out mildly. "I pick where we go."

"Right." She pushed her glasses down and gave him a look. "I did Rose Wall earlier, so diving with the sea lions is a nice site to pair with that dive."

The breeze picked up over the water just enough to plaster her T-shirt against her body. Today's bikini was yellow with white daisies. And she was definitely cold.

No. Don't go there. Friday night's hot sex had been an aberration. Getting him out of her system. That's what Piper had called it. And he was okay with that. She'd taken him to bed, had her way with him for one wicked night, and now it was over. It didn't matter if parts of him were interested in a repeat.

"Do you plan on asking me for my list?" He wondered if she'd admit she'd planned on commandeering their joint project and choosing their sites for both of them.

"I can guess what's on it. You've probably got three superdeep sites requiring four advance certifications and a secret life as a military ninja." She pushed her glasses up and lay back. "Tell me I'm wrong."

"You're wrong," he said promptly. "I've got four sites on my list."

"Do you really think the Fiesta execs are going to be up for advanced dives?"

"Trust me. Ninja certification is not required."

"Did you ask any of them if they were certified? Or what their comfort levels were?"

"I didn't hear you ask them those questions," he pointed out. "And I reviewed their logbooks."

"My dives are easy."

Unlike the woman sitting in front of him. Piper was the exact opposite of easy. She was prickly, argumentative, and, yeah, he liked it. She kept him on his toes. She was also a whole lot of fun, starting with the way she was ignoring him. Friday night had been amazing, and he still had his night in charge to look forward to. Cal was fairly certain the entire island had spotted the chemistry between the two of them by now. All through brunch on Saturday, his mother had dropped overt hints to bring Piper by for a family dinner. "Soon," she'd emphasized.

Since it was his boat and he had the wheel, overruling Piper wasn't difficult. He let her talk and then he laid in a course for Devil's Slide anyhow. She lounged in the front of the boat, chattering away about yesterday's sites and the joys of swimming with sea lion pups (none of which Cal found particularly convincing). Listening to her talk wasn't a hardship. Her face lit up and she waved her hands around, as if she was conducting an invisible symphony. The logical thing to do would have been to tell her where they were really going, but he didn't want the fight.

By the time they were halfway to Piper's first site, however, his nerves were shot. All he wanted was to turn the boat around and head back to the marina. He'd tried a quick phone call earlier in the day to see if the Fiesta team would let him switch himself out for Tag or Daeg, but that approach had been a no-go. Fiesta wanted to see him leading his program.

He wanted to see the same thing, probably more than anyone.

Piper looked back at him and grinned. Her sunglasses were covered with the spray the boat had kicked up and she looked as if there was nowhere else she'd rather be.

"We've got a perfect day," she called over the noise of

the motor, sounding like she meant it. Of course, she didn't have any issues diving. In fact, if she knew what he knew, she might be smiling even wider because he was going to lose. And she was going to win.

Think of this as a dry run, he told himself. It doesn't have to be perfect—it just has to happen. Suddenly too hot, he stripped off his T-shirt. Piper slid him a look from over her sunglasses that only heated him up further.

Which was good.

Remembering their night together definitely took his mind off the upcoming dive. And...there it was. Adrenaline punched through his body in a sickening rush. The chemical rush taunted him with visions of failure as his head spun a thousand different scenarios in which he wasn't able to do this.

The U.S. Navy SEALs trained a man to react well under pressure. Pressure like jumping fins first out of a Blackhawk into stormy water or searching an enemy bay for underwater explosives. He'd done those things and more, so he could handle one practice dive. He'd go under, and there'd be nothing lurking below the surface, waiting to kill him. It would be just him and Piper.

Everything would be fine.

He inhaled. Exhaled. Repeated the process while he did his best not to drive the boat off course.

Piper accidentally rescued him. When the cliffs rose up in front of them and he throttled back to guide the dive boat around the breakwater and into the sheltered cove, she knew exactly where they were. Or *weren't*.

She sat up. "This is not Pup Alley."

It also wasn't the marina, where he desperately wanted to be. "My turn," he reminded her when she eyed the site. *He hoped.*

They both knew she hadn't put this on her list. The

site was known both for its difficult entry and thrilling exit. Divers entered by jumping off the cliff. After that, things got deep, fast. There were plenty of barracuda plus the occasional shark. After the dive, participants timed the incoming waves and rode one over the rocky ledge to shoot into the sheltered cove. Chickening out of that ride meant a mile-long swim around the breakwater. Cal had dived the site every chance he'd gotten on previous visits to the island.

She muttered something he didn't catch, but he figured she'd bring up whatever it was again later. Probably more than once. He bit back a smile.

Twenty minutes later, he wasn't smiling, and the marina was definitely looking better and better. They'd anchored the boat a few feet offshore, unloaded the gear and walked through the dive plan. The slog up the path to the top of the cliff had taken far less time than Cal remembered, even with the necessity of loading the dive tanks into the hand-cranked elevator running up the side of the cliff.

"Are you sure?" she asked, walking over to the edge and peering down. She didn't look bothered by the height or the difficulty of the dive he'd proposed. On the other hand, Piper could probably go face-to-face with a shark and keep her cool.

The screaming of the gulls overhead had him on edge, almost as much as the relentless slap of the waves against the rocks. No, he wasn't sure. He also knew his nerves were a mental game his head was playing with his body. And, when he looked over the edge at the churning water, he was pretty certain his head was winning.

Piper backed away from the edge. Thank God. "After you," she said.

He couldn't.

His head kept running scenarios where she went under

and didn't come up, his heart pounding out an alarm with each unwelcome image. If he couldn't be there for her, if he couldn't guarantee he'd see to her safety then…he couldn't dive.

"Piper."

"Yeah?"

"I—" What did he say? How did he tell her that something bad had happened but he, conditioned SEAL and expert diver, hadn't been able to wrap his head around it? He looked at the surface, imagined going under, and it was as though someone had cut the air to his brain.

"Come on." She turned and strode back to the top of the path. Also known as the walk of shame. When he didn't immediately head down the trail, she stopped walking, waiting for him to catch up. Good thing she hadn't tried a wait-and-see move in the water, because he could admit to himself that he would have failed her. If she'd had trouble, he wouldn't have been there for her, and that bothered him even more than his jacked-up head did.

He was pathetic.

"How'd it happen?"

He didn't have to ask what the "it" was.

"One bad mission and now I can't dive." The words hung in the air behind them. "I can jump off the cliff, but when I descend…it's all shit." He wasn't sure what he expected her to do. She couldn't fix this, either, and it was his mess anyhow.

"I noticed." When he risked a look at her, she didn't look pitying—just accepting.

He scrubbed a hand over his head. Daeg and Tag certainly knew, as well. Apparently the Fiesta cruise execs were the only ones who hadn't gotten the memo.

"Maybe we can work through it." She bumped her shoulder lightly against his.

"Some things can't be fixed," he said. *And some things had to be said.*

"We'll try." She threaded her fingers through his and tugged him forward. Screw it. He let her.

"Not being able to dive is a pretty big liability for a dive master."

The beach rose up before them as she murmured her agreement—and he was fairly certain she owed her curse jar another round of quarters—and strode toward the water.

"Sit," she demanded, dropping to the sand right above the waterline.

Since she didn't let go of his hand, he followed. Okay, he was also curious to see where she'd take this conversation and, since he wasn't diving today, he had plenty of time. He sincerely doubted she could do anything about his unwelcome phobia but he already knew Piper didn't know the meaning of the word *quit*.

Piper...

She'd taken a devastating hit to her knee, a career-ending injury. She didn't look unhappy, though. On the contrary. She'd healed and then she'd come back to Discovery Island and started over. He didn't know if he had that in him, but he admired her tenacity. She made up her mind about what she wanted and she went for it. Her head was definitely on straight, unlike his. Which made him wonder why she was out here with him. If she hadn't known before, she knew now. He wouldn't be leading any diving trips for the Fiesta Cruise Lines' folks.

"What exactly bothers you about diving?" Their hands, he couldn't help but notice, were still connected. The waves washed in, swirling around their feet before retreating. "You clearly don't have a problem with getting wet. And you used up all the hot water at my place, by the way."

"Nope." He was A-OK with that part of diving. And with showering at her place.

"So, which specific part don't you like?" She wiggled a little, digging into the sand with her butt, and the move had her shoulder brushing against his. Then, because apparently that wasn't torture enough, she reached up and unzipped her wet suit. The black Neoprene rubber parted, revealing a sun-kissed V of skin. The daisies on her bikini top winked mockingly at him.

He gritted his teeth. "I panic when I submerge."

"That must have been one heck of a mission." Score one for Piper.

When he didn't say anything, though, she poked him in the side. "Confession's good for the soul."

He'd never believed that. "The mission went…south." She poked him again. "Jesus, Piper. You're not helping."

"I'd like to." Her voice turned unexpectedly serious. "But you have to let me, Cal."

Right.

"Have you discussed this with Daeg and Tag? Or with your family? A trained professional?"

"No," he said curtly. "This is something I have to get over. It's not something anyone else can fix."

"The first time I climbed the diving tower after my accident, I told myself everything would be fine. A nice, easy forward pike. Nothing too complicated or twisty. The minute I made my approach, though, I knew I was in trouble. My knee didn't have any intention of cooperating. My power leg took the hit in the accident, and I didn't get any height off the board. I told myself it was just one dive, so I tried it again. Same story." She shrugged. "Every time I climbed the tower."

"So you quit." As soon as the words were out, he wished he could take it back. A look of pain flashed across her face, quickly masked. Piper didn't like it when other people saw her hurting. She'd been like that the day he'd pulled her out of the water, too, insisting she was fine even though she'd been out of her head with pain and shock.

"I thought of it as moving on."

"I'm not ready to let go of this," he said quietly.

Acting on impulse, he reached down and touched her knee. She'd chosen to wear a shorty rather than a full wet suit, and for the first time, he wondered if she'd known there was no way he was diving. The scar on her knee was a thick, twisted ridge. No matter how much sun she got, the scar tissue would always stay white. He ran a finger along the side of her leg.

"Does it hurt?"

"Not unless I overdo it. Or wear three-inch heels for hours on end."

"I wish I could have done something more."

She was silent for a moment. "Me, too, but you did everything you could." She splashed him, knocking water onto him with the flat of her hand. "You're holding out on me. Spill."

"I'm not going to melt."

"Or run shrieking?" There was something about the look in her eyes as she slid him a sidelong glance. Piper being playful wasn't new. He'd watched her pull this shit for years, poking, teasing, prodding. She had no fear and no boundaries. And yet, right now he was okay with it. He didn't mind her asking.

Okay. Scratch that. He minded a whole lot, but he sensed that the reasons behind the questions were well-intentioned. She wasn't asking in order to make fun of him. Nope. Piper wanted to help.

Him.

Something tightened in the region of his heart. "I won't run," he agreed.

"Good." She bumped his shoulder companionably with hers again, a little smile playing across her lips. Like they were old friends, but…he didn't want to be friends with Piper. Or, rather, he didn't *just* want to be friends with her. He looked at her and saw the same face, the same person, he'd known since he was ten, but now he saw someone more. A woman he wanted to get to know better. Piper was more than a pretty face and a bum knee, or even a stubborn, argumentative competitor.

"You're smiling," she said, but her eyes were firmly fixed on the ocean.

"You bet."

"We already did," she said darkly.

"And I paid up."

"Which makes it my turn," she pointed out. "I owe you a night."

One more wicked night with Piper. Just the thought had his body heating up, but he didn't want to go to bed with Piper because of a bet, either. Not that he wasn't grateful for the cover story. He had a feeling that the chemistry between them had been as much of a surprise to her as it had to him. One night hadn't erased the attraction.

He still wanted Piper.

And, after he ran the logic in his head for a moment, he didn't imagine his feelings were going to change after the good folks at the Fiesta Cruise Lines awarded their contract.

"Tell me more," she repeated, leaning against him. "Tell me it all."

He shook his head. "I wish it were that simple, Piper."

"I'm waiting," was all she said.

She really was going to make him say it.

He risked a look at her face, but she didn't look horrified or shocked. He read concern there, but it seemed more directed at him and less, "I'm partnered with a crazy man." She chewed on her lower lip, clearly thinking something through.

"We were on a rescue mission over the Indian Ocean, searching for survivors from a tsunami that had hit the area hard. Whole villages had been sucked out to sea, and sometimes, if we were lucky, there were survivors clinging to the debris. We'd already pulled two people up in the basket, but the water was rough and there was enough crap in it to be a concern."

It wasn't the chop that got to you. It was the unseen obstacles in churned-up water. You couldn't see. All you could do was swim and pray—and get the survivors into the basket as fast as possible. They'd plucked two people off an impromptu raft that looked like it might have been the wall of a house or a shed door. Whatever it was, it was unrecognizable now, but it floated and it had made all the difference to the two survivors.

"I'd come up with the first survivor, and Daeg and Lars went down to get the second. They'd gotten their guy into the basket, but Daeg took a hit. Lars convinced him to go up first."

Cal could see that rescue as if it were yesterday.

THE BASKET CAME up in slow motion, like things did in nightmares but weren't supposed to do in real life. Cal reached for the metal frame, steadying it as it bumped against the edge of the chopper, and they prepared to haul it in. For just a moment, he took his eyes off his boys in the water and focused on getting the survivor out and into the comparative safety of the chopper. The guy was in shock—no surprise after forty hours at sea—and didn't or couldn't speak English. Since Cal's Hindi consisted of yes, no, and "Where's the bar?" his linguistic efforts weren't helping to calm the guy down, either. Although maybe the guy could have used a drink. Cal knew how he'd have felt after being sucked out to sea by a tsunami.

And then the pilot cursed over the headset. Screw international diplomacy. Cal picked up the survivor and set him down on a jump seat, buckling the safety harness around him.

"What do we have?"

He moved for the open bay door, looked down and... spotted blood in the water. A pool of crimson spread out around Daeg, even as the spotter barked out a terse announcement. "Houston, we have ourselves a problem."

They sure did. No way could Daeg make it up the ladder, dangling from the chopper, so Cal sent the basket back down. It seemed to take twice as long to reach the ocean's surface as it had on the previous trip, but he knew that was an illusion. Time hadn't really slowed to a crawl. He'd reach Daeg in time.

As soon as the basket was down, Lars loaded Daeg in. Cal assumed strong-arming was involved. The basket was for survivors and not for SEALs. Daeg would be razzed about his ride for months.

Cal grinned, relief washing over him, and then, just like that, Lars disappeared. One minute he was treading water, his hand holding on to the ladder as he waited for the basket to clear, and then he was gone. They'd dropped the chopper lower, searching. He couldn't tell if the water was clear or not, but Lars wasn't on the surface. He'd jumped, mask on, arms crossed and fins down. He couldn't get down there quickly enough, ripping through the water's surface and mentally sectioning the area into quadrants.

No Lars.

Nothing but brown churn from the tsunami and the cyclone. All the picture-postcard blue was gone, and he was diving in a garbage dump. Boards and trees and wood. Pieces of fishing boats, netting and what had to be the contents of a half-dozen villages. Animals and who knew what else.

Dive. Surface. Over and over, until the chopper ran dangerously low on fuel.

He'd ascended, leaving Lars out there somewhere. He'd have gladly traded his own life for the other man's, but destiny wasn't willing to broker the deal. He'd lost a brother, when there should have been something he could do to rescue him. Like his job. Years of training, thousands of mission hours rescuing others, but he'd come up short on the most important rescue of them all.

"ANOTHER TEAM RETRIEVED Lars's body a day later. All I have left of him now are his tags." He fisted the tags around his neck.

By his side, Piper didn't make the uh-huh noises or the head nods. She sat there silently, taking in his words, but her shoulder pressed against his arm, her fingers stayed tangled up with his in the sand. He fought the urge to press her down and strip off her clothes. To lose both himself and the memories in Piper. That wasn't fair to her, though, and he didn't deserve the escape.

After, when he'd told her what he remembered, there was silence. He concentrated on his breathing, the regular in and out of air moving through his lungs the same way the waves came in and then retreated. One breath. Inhale and hold for twenty. Exhale, and then a second. And a third. Eventually, she snuck a peek at him. He was pretty sure he didn't look okay, because the pressure on his arm got deeper, and then she stood up.

"Can you swim with me?" she asked. "Not a dive," she added quickly.

He had a sudden feeling he might follow Piper just about anywhere. He filed the thought away to consider later.

"I can swim. I train every day."

She nodded, and he could practically see the gears turning in her head as she considered various ideas. He didn't need her to fix him, which was a good thing because he had a sneaking suspicion he was broken beyond all repair. Or that it was going to take years he didn't have before the Fiesta demonstration. She reached down and held out a hand.

"You're still sitting down," she teased.

Warmth unfolded in him.

When he took her hand, she eyed him cautiously. They did have history, after all. "You're not going to pull me in, are you?"

She'd done that to him on more than one occasion. She reacted first, thought later. He tightened his fingers on hers and her eyes narrowed.

"Nope," he said. "Although I reserve the right to do so later."

She grinned. "There's hope for you yet, Cal."

He hoped so. He really, really hoped so.

PIPER HAD ALWAYS had nothing but respect for the men and women who chose to serve. She couldn't imagine flying away and leaving a man down because it was the right thing to do. Because otherwise the people you'd come out to rescue would be jeopardized. Those kinds of decisions didn't come up in her life—and probably explained Cal's fanatic insistence on staying safe.

She tugged and zipped as they waded in, grateful for the shorty's insulation. Although the water here was shallow enough that the sun had warmed up the surface, it still packed quite a chill. The ocean off the California coast was definitely no South Pacific dream when it came to warmth, although it didn't seem to bother Cal. Maybe it was his SEAL training.

Piper waded until she was chest deep, then sank down lower and lower into the water. Cal stopped with her, letting her set the pace.

"Thank you."

"That's what friends are for." She said the words lightly.

"Are we?" He rested his forehead against hers.

Were they? She thought about it for a moment, and the answer was yes. In a strange, frenemy kind of way, Cal was her friend. He was arrogant and pigheaded, and she'd probably butt heads with him when she was ninety but... yeah. They were friends. Returning to Discovery Island had proved Cal had redeeming qualities, if nothing else.

"I think so."

The next small wave picked her up, bumping her against Cal. He was taller than she was, and his legs easily reached the bottom here. Plus, his larger body mass made it harder for the waves to knock him around. Taking advantage of his relative stability, she wrapped her legs around his waist, anchoring herself. And, okay, enjoying the heck out of the close contact, too. She grabbed for his shoulders with her hands.

"Because this seems more like kiss and make up," he said.

"You don't kiss your friends?"

"I could make an exception."

Cal needed a friend. It was something about his eyes, she decided. He had gorgeous eyes, the rich brown making her think of decadent treats like brownies and chocolate. Usually, there was more than a hint of reserve in his eyes.

Or disapproval. Cal didn't wear his heart on his sleeve. He liked being in control. Right now, though, her SEAL looked more than a little lost.

Admitting to a weakness wasn't something he did. She understood. She really did, because she was the same way. She leaned in closer and his hands cupped her butt, helping her out. They both were all about showing a strong front to the world. When she'd still been diving competitively, she'd known that even a bad dive meant she climbed out of the pool with her game face on. Don't show the cameras, the people in the stands or the other divers how much the entry had hurt or that she knew she'd over-rotated. Keep it to yourself. Do the postmortem later, over and over, making sure the mistake never happened again.

Cal blamed himself for his teammate's death. She'd bet he hadn't discussed it with Tag and Daeg—and that they all carried around their own burdens of guilt. She wondered why guys couldn't mention the word *feelings* without clamming up, but then another wave pushed her higher in Cal's arms. His thumb stroked the curve of her butt.

"Make me the exception?" she suggested, her mouth inches from his. She couldn't fix him, as much as she wanted to, any more than he could undo the damage the Jet Ski accident had done to her knee. So here they were, two people who were used to being in charge and making things better, and neither of them knew what to do with the other.

Okay. She had one idea.

"You bet," he said roughly.

Good enough.

The ocean pushed her against him. That was the excuse she gave herself as she pressed her mouth against his.

He didn't pull back. Instead, eyes open, he stared at her with single-minded intensity. His grip on her butt tightened as his eyes drifted closed. It was strange. This was *Cal,* for crying out loud, and she'd never imagined she'd be kissing him. And yet she was.

And he was kissing her back.

"Piper," he said roughly, her name half laugh, half groan, as he tore his mouth away from hers.

"You've got my name right," she agreed. "Kiss me some more."

And he did.

His mouth covered hers as he settled in, his tongue tangling with hers as she made a greedy sound. Her hands cupped his head, her thumbs tracing the pulse banging in his neck as they sank lower and lower in the water.

He knew what she was doing. He'd tried the same thing in the bathtub, and his head had no problem with a few inches of clean, soapy water. It was the open ocean and what hid beneath the surface that did him in. Still, he appreciated the effort.

He had his feet firmly planted on the sand. They had no masks, no tanks. The odd rock on the bottom made itself felt through the bottom of his dive booties, but her fingers gripped his shoulders, gripped him. See? This was okay.

When she tore her mouth from his, they were both breathing hard.

"So far, so good?"

"Yeah," he agreed jaggedly.

"Focus on me." Her mouth closed over his again, and this time she took them under with a kiss, gently pushing down beneath the surface. One foot. Two. His brain refused to shut off, counting off the distance between him and the surface.

Something brushed his thigh, and he startled. *Piper.* His eyes flew open, stinging in the salt water, but she was right there. He wanted to give her what they both wanted—

a miraculous insta-cure for his phobia—but instead he settled for slowly floating them both back to the surface.

He hadn't panicked.

That had to count for something.

"You think the Fiesta folks would like a dive like that?"

She shot him a naughty grin. "Margie Kemp might."

Right. The female member of the Fiesta team. "You don't think I'm Sal's type?"

He felt her shudder. "He must be *someone's* type," she answered, but she sounded doubtful.

"Not mine," he said.

He rolled and swam lazily for shore. She clung playfully to his shoulders, riding his back.

"You should talk with someone."

No. What he needed was to do something. To *fix* this. He'd spent one minute five feet underwater. He'd served as a U.S. Navy SEAL. He'd swum despite near hypothermia, powered through two-mile swims with his fins dragging at his feet. He'd made combat swims that were still classified and dived into storm-churned water from a Blackhawk.

Five feet didn't begin to cut it.

And yet she'd tried and that mattered. "Thanks. For—" Too bad he didn't have a list of words. He wanted her to know he appreciated what she'd done, but neither of them had spent much timing talking about feelings or mouthing "thank you."

"I only wish I was a miracle worker."

Apparently, though, she got it.

"You are," he said roughly. She had no idea. When he focused on *her,* he wasn't focused on the dive. His head stayed in the game just a little more, and he dived just a little farther. Hell, with another hundred sessions or so of kiss therapy, he might make it to a full twenty feet.

He slogged out of the water and onto the beach.

"Can Daeg or Tag lead your dives?"

He'd suggested the switch. "Fiesta insists I do it."

"Right." There was a pause. Clearly, she understood exactly what that meant for his chances of landing the contract. "All right," she said. "I just want you to know I've got your back. If there's anything I can do, count me in, okay?"

And…now he felt lower than low. She had his back—and he'd placed a bid on her place. Telling her was suddenly more important than ever because, even if he hadn't known the dive shop he was offering for belonged to her in part, he knew *now*. On the other hand, he wasn't going to seal the deal on the Fiesta contract. It wouldn't matter.

"Okay?" she asked.

He wanted to be. More than anything.

"You bet," he said and led the way back to the boat.

12

THE DIVE BOAT slapped and bounced over the waves when Daeg opened the throttle and let her rip. Piper had played and replayed this afternoon in her head a million times, as she had countless numbers of platform dives. She would imagine how something was going to unfold, step by step, and then her body would step through the sequence flawlessly, even when nerves froze her head.

Leading the Fiesta crew through her dive had been an adrenaline rush. Later, she'd do a postmortem with Carla, but right now she was fiercely happy. The dive had gone well. Better than well. She and Carla had partnered with Cal and Daeg to lead the day's demonstration dives. Since Piper's dive was technically less challenging, they'd opted to do hers first in case the Fiesta crew turned out to have any issues diving. They'd motored slowly past one of the smaller islands close to Discovery Island where the sea lions congregated.

Even before they'd spotted the sea lion colony, raucous barking had competed with the harsher cry of the gulls. Up close, the sea lions were awkwardly cute, pulling themselves across the sand on their flippers. The creatures also had more things to say to each other than a houseful of Brennans. The noise was deafening.

After walking the divers through the site and performing gear checks, she'd rolled off the side of the boat. Underwater, her field of vision exploded into a sea of miniature bubbles as she tucked and rolled, swimming smoothly to the anchor line just off the dive boat's prow. The other divers had followed, with Cal staying behind on board to monitor the surface and keep an eye on the boat.

Even before she'd signaled their descent, they'd had a clear view of the dozens of sea lions diving through the water around them. The animals had been perfectly happy to swim with the divers, had spiraled through the kelp forest and over to the edge where the bottom dropped away steeply in a trail of bubbles. When they'd surfaced forty minutes later, working their way slowly up the safety line, the Fiesta team had been excited. Carla had taken photographs of them and, as she'd passed the camera around, the group had relaxed with bottles of water and sliced watermelon.

The mature thing to do would be to play it cool and not rub Cal's face in the spectacular success her dive had been. But…screw it. She was one step closer to winning this competition, and they both knew it.

She leaned up and whispered in his ear, "Beat that."

Do-or-die time.

Cal pulled the dive boat into the cove behind Devil's Slide, and everybody piled onto the beach for the day's second dive. Piper and Daeg got busy unloading tanks and gear, while Cal walked the divers through the site. Being this close to Piper on what he might have started calling their beach—words he wouldn't admit out loud—was distracting. He kept remembering how she'd wrapped herself around him in the surf. The way she'd just been there for him, with him. And, of course, her kiss. He remembered all of their kisses and not because there hadn't been enough of them.

Five kisses.

One at the Pleasure Pier. The second on today's beach. He'd kissed Piper right there where he'd anchored the dive boat. He'd also had three kisses—four, he decided—the night she'd decided they were going to bed together. Those kisses had been marathon kisses and might count for more, except they hadn't come up for air. If he was lucky, he'd up their kiss count today. He was aiming to break into double digits.

Thinking about Piper right now was crazy. She had every intention of kicking his butt in this competition, and he'd all but handed her the win anyhow. He had to go in the water in ten minutes and lead five divers through the Devil's Slide. Kissing wasn't part of his plan.

Plus, he had no idea what would happen to them after the Fiesta competition wrapped. If he won the contract, he lost Piper. He didn't kid himself. Piper played to win. She'd made her position perfectly clear. She was outrageous, impulsive and dedicated. His SEAL training had taught him to value the kind of determination to do whatever it took to get the job done.

Sal Britten, the senior Fiesta executive, spouted off as they made the all-too-short climb to the top of the cliff. Cal had checked the guy's logbook. Twice. Sal Britten had dived some pretty world-renowned sites. Cal just wished the guy would shut up. He was pompous and arrogant, sure he knew more about diving than either of the two dive masters leading the trip.

And he was also vocal in sharing his knowledge. He'd critiqued the boat, the tanks, the shorties and the amount of weight Cal had added to his belt. Pushing the guy off the cliff, while satisfying, would be a major ethical violation, but Cal was seriously tempted. From the way Piper's mouth twitched as Sal finished describing the wall dive he'd done in Tahiti two months ago, she felt the same way.

And…showtime.

While Carla and Piper helped Ben and Margie, the other two Fiesta divers, into their harnesses and tanks, Cal walked over to the edge of the cliff. It was every bit as far to the surface as he'd remembered. If his only problem had been the height, he'd have been golden. Piper would be happy to shove him over.

He still had no idea how he was going to do this.

Daeg came over and stared down at the ocean waiting at the bottom of the cliff. "You got this?"

Unfortunately, Cal knew what the other man was asking. He wasn't stupid. He'd known Daeg would pick up on his issues with diving. As long as Cal's issues had been personal, Daeg had backed off. He hadn't pressed, which Cal appreciated. When those same issues came into play with a mission, however, Daeg had to ask questions.

So, the question was: did he?

Mentally he walked through the dive. Forty-five minutes from when his feet left the cliff top until he waded back out on the beach. Four people counting on him. He couldn't jump unless he knew he could lead the dive, and he felt uncertain. Okay. Scratch that. He felt with heart-stopping certainty that diving now would be a big mistake.

"I can lead the dive." He wasn't surprised to find Piper standing next to him. "We'll tell Fiesta you had to dive last night for a rescue and that you're still in the no-dive window because they moved up their dive times today."

He wanted to get this right. Hell, he *needed* to get this

right. He knew Piper felt the same way, and yet she was offering to cover for him.

"That what you want?" Daeg loaded weights into his own belt. Without the weight, Daeg would shoot right back to the surface, and it would be dive over.

"Trust me on this one," Piper said, her eyes watching his. "I've got your back. I'll get this right for you."

Strangely, he believed her. Staying out of the water was the safe thing to do. The *right* thing to do.

"You dive," he agreed.

She flashed him a grin. "I'm thinking you owe me at least one more night."

Sal strode up then, already talking, talking, talking as he waited for Piper to buddy check his gear. At least the man would have to shut up once he had his regulator in.

Piper raised an eyebrow.

"Two," Cal mouthed. Of course, not diving with Sal was probably worth at least a week, but some things a man didn't admit.

Diving with Sal was a nightmare.

Piper made a mental note to kill Cal when she surfaced. Two nights were nowhere near enough compensation for Sal's boorish behavior. First, the guy had rechecked all of his gear after she'd done a buddy check on him. He'd insisted on adding more weight to his belt and then he'd taken issue with the gauge on his tank, insisting the device was faulty and blustering loudly until Carla switched it out.

Things hadn't improved once they were in the water, either, when at least talking became impossible. Instead of sticking near her, he'd swum all over the place, checking out whatever interested him and completely ignoring her. He desperately needed a refresher course in dive safety, but fifty feet down was not the classroom she had in mind.

The site was as gorgeous as Cal had promised. In addition to the caves dotting the underside of the cliff, colorful gorgonians and anemones covered the rugged underwater slope, and a spectacular kelp forest sheltered hundreds of bluefish. She'd also spotted at least five different kinds of starfish, including sun stars and blood stars. Schools of bright orange garibaldi flashed around them. Since it wasn't nesting season, they didn't have to worry about overly aggressive daddy fish attacking them. She'd always appreciated their sense of family, but she and Cal needed today's dive to be perfect.

Thirty-five minutes of show-and-tell later, and it was time for Devil's Slide. Divers had to time their approach to the rocky ledge to correspond with the incoming waves. The added push would send them shooting over the lip and into the calmer interior bay. Then it was a simple swim to the boat. Cliff jump, admire the anemones, explore the underwater caves and then shoot the pass. Cal clearly liked a good adventure dive.

Daeg signaled as they huddled together, pulling out his dive slate. Margie, the Fiesta exec, was going to pass on shooting the chute. She'd take the longer surface swim over the adrenaline rush of the quicker exit. Piper nodded. Better to go the long way 'round if Margie wasn't confident about the approach. After a quick air check, Daeg and Margie swam off, leaving Carla, Piper and their two divers.

She signaled for Carla to go up first with her diver and go through the chute, while she and Sal remained on the bottom. Cal, she had to admit, had picked a lovely site, all pink, cream and gold fans and strands of kelp. The waves coming in and going out created a graceful ballet, everything dancing around them as they waited for their turn to ascend.

The Fiesta team had to be eating this up.

Ben disappeared into the chute overhead, riding the waves over the ledge. Carla flashed a thumbs-up and then circled around to time her ride. Eyes intent on the action overhead, Sal bumped into a patch of fans, startling a young horn shark hiding inside. The shark was a nice specimen, almost three feet long, brown-and-white speckled with the trademark fin. Its tail cut through the water, propelling the shark away from them at lightning speed.

Nice. Cal's dive had produced sharks, too. Good thing she'd had all that sea lion cuteness or she'd be seriously worried right now. This dive was good stuff. Just in case Sal had missed the shark sighting, she pointed, but Sal had clearly already seen. He scrambled backward, hyperventilating.

Horn sharks often hung out in the algae beds off Discovery Island, and Cal had briefed them about the remote possibility of seeing the sharks during the dive. Since horn sharks preferred to hunt for shellfish at night, they hid out during the daytime, resting. Divers formed no part of their dining menu, so Sal had nothing to worry about. It wasn't like he'd just come face to snout with a Great White.

Either he hadn't been listening, however, when Cal had walked them through what they might see at the site, or he'd forgotten. He was also going to empty his tank if he kept sucking air in so hard. As if he'd read her mind, he reached behind him, clearly having decided he wasn't getting enough air and twisted the valve on his tank, cranking hard.

An enormous spray of bubbles exploded from his regulator as she reached his side and laid a hand on his arm. She could hear him gasping for breath and then there was a second explosion of bubbles, followed by a third as Sal started to hyperventilate. Grabbing her arm, he made a panicked, twisting motion with his hand, signaling he was out of air.

Not good.

The first rule of diving safety was to calm down and assess. She looked up. Carla's diver disappeared into the chute, driving hard with his fins, but Carla circled, clearly torn between descending again to assist and sticking with her dive buddy. Piper had been so focused on an oarfish once, that she'd accidentally held her breath and hyperventilated. What Sal was experiencing was no fun. Because he wasn't exhaling completely, his lungs were holding on to stale, used air. Then, when he inhaled, he only got part of a breath.

Unfortunately, he wasn't helping her to help him. He thrashed away from her, his fins drilling into her legs. She'd bruise tomorrow, but bruises weren't the problem. She needed to calm him down and then get him to the surface. She finally caught a peek at his gauge and, holy trouble, Batman. He'd turned the valve the wrong way and was dangerously low on gas.

She pointed to the bottom, and his eyes widened almost comically. He wanted to ascend *now.* She understood, but if he went up too fast from fifty feet, he'd have a date with the decompression chamber. Sal was a pompous, arrogant windbag, but she wouldn't wish a case of the bends on her worst enemy. Unfortunately, he looked like he was beyond reason.

She sank down to the bottom, tugging on him. If she could get him to kneel, she could at least close his valve and salvage any remaining gas while she got him to buddy breathe with her, but he kept on twisting away from her, trying to keep the shark in his line of vision. Grabbing her dive slate, she scrawled, "Stop. Kneel. I've got you."

Her answer was another hard explosion of bubbles, Sal's

labored breathing filling her ears as he grabbed for her regulator, clearly determined to fix this problem for himself.

AT PRECISELY FORTY-FIVE minutes, Carla popped to the surface. Cal checked his watch. She'd sped up her ascent. Behind her, Ben surfaced.

"I need another tank," Carla yelled, swimming hard for the boat.

Nope. He'd heard wrong. Carla was done for the day, so why would she need more gas? He eyeballed the area. There was no sign of Daeg yet, but he'd mentioned earlier that his diver might not try shooting the chute. He *didn't* see Piper and Sal, however, and the nonsighting was a problem. His senses went on full alert.

"What's the issue?" He reached down a hand to help her board.

"Piper's guy ran out of air."

Sal outweighed Piper almost two to one. He'd be a heavy breather anyhow, and if he panicked… Cal should have gone. He should have known Sal was going to be nothing but trouble. Instead, he'd let Piper step in for him.

"If they have to buddy breathe, they'll take the longer surface swim. I'm going to jump with another tank so we can speed that process up."

"I'll go," he said.

Falling into a mission mindset was easy. Stop. Assess. Act. Moving rapidly, he grabbed gear, loading the lift swiftly before flying up the path, forcing the air in and out of his lungs in a steady rhythm. He wouldn't be any good to Piper and Sal if he winded himself. At the top, Carla helped him gear up, her eyes scanning the ocean below them.

"I still don't see them," she said. "They should have surfaced inside the bay or out."

"Walk me through it." He moved to the edge.

Jumping was the easy part. The part after was the problem. Carla hesitated, her hand on his tank.

"Are you okay?" she asked.

She was female and she'd dived twice today. Neither of them needed him to point out that her build put her at a disadvantage in this race. He was bigger and he was fresh. Carrying double tanks wasn't a challenge for him—and it was his job, his contract, his…Piper down there.

He nodded. "I'm good."

"Okay. We dived, and Piper led us through the course you'd mapped up. We were at the final meeting point, taking turns ascending, when Sal ran into a problem. Based on what I saw, I'm guessing he ran low on air and hyperventilated."

There was still no sign of divers on the surface, but he couldn't see the open water where Daeg and his companion were.

"You're good." Carla slapped his shoulder. "She's probably got this, but—"

But taking the chance was stupid. Normally, he'd stick with the boat, maybe motor around to see if he could spot them, but a two-hundred-twenty-pound man with a chip on his shoulder and no air was a recipe for disaster.

He stepped onto the edge.

Looked down.

Big mistake. He'd dived from this cliff dozens, if not hundreds, of times before, but his head was reminding him that he couldn't dive anymore, and his legs locked up, refusing to take him past the edge. Once he jumped, there was no do over. No going back. With the weight belt and the double tanks, he'd sink hard and fast. He didn't want to jump, but that was his head talking. His heart knew right where he belonged. He couldn't stay out of the water when Piper was risking it all.

"Get back to the boat," he said to Carla. "Bring it around the breakwater. Keep an eye out for Daeg and Margie, and I'll bring Sal and Piper to the surface wherever they are."

"Got it." She hesitated and then stepped back. "Good luck."

One. Two.

On three, he stepped off the edge of the cliff.

Going down was the easy part. Gravity did all the work. All he had to do was keep his flippers pointed down and his arms crossed over his chest. Oh, and not think about what was coming next. He ripped through the surface and sank fast, the extra weight on his belt pulling him down.

Ten feet. Fifteen. He spotted, trying to orient himself and…cue the panic. His heart raced and he gulped air, his fingers going numb. Breathe, he reminded himself. Breathe and count. One. He passed twenty feet, his descent slowing. Two. His heartbeat deafened him, his chest constricting. Four. Piper smiling as she rode the swing ride. Five. Piper on the back of his Harley. Six. Piper on his kitchen counter. So, okay, that one hadn't happened yet, but a man could dream. He forced himself deeper.

SPOTS DANCED IN front of her eyes. Chest burning, she reached for her regulator, but Sal wasn't in a sharing mood. He jammed her regulator into his mouth and breathed frantically. Her tank was running dangerously light now, too. She stretched for her alternate air supply, hooking her fingers around the secondary regulator.

The thing was Sal had to calm down. Shooting the slide with him wasn't an option—even if he hadn't been in full-blown panic mode, safely positioning two divers sharing a single tank was out of the question. Her best bet was to get him to surface in a controlled ascent. Carla would alert Cal, and the dive boat could come around and pick them up.

The shark picked that moment to peek back out from its kelp refuge, and Sal started jettisoning weights from his belt. *Darn it.* If he made an emergency ascent too quickly and without the required safety stops, he'd definitely be paying a visit to the decompression chamber on the mainland.

She needed help.

A second tank.

Or, hey, since she was brainstorming, a big stick to knock some sense into Sal. She needed to breathe, and she needed to get Sal to the surface, but the man wasn't letting her get on with either job.

Sal jerked hard on her harness a second time, clearly intending to take her—or her air supply—with him. Yeah. Good luck, since she was still harnessed in.

Big hands reached around her. Thank God, the cavalry had arrived. Piper had never been so glad that Cal was a big man. He effortlessly manhandled Sal away from her, inserting his body between them as he held up a small, bright yellow tank and regulator. He motioned for Sal to put the regulator in his mouth. As soon as the other man did, Cal activated the bottle of emergency air.

He'd brought a spare for her, too, and she gladly switched over to it. While he reweighted Sal, who was sucking on the backup air, she checked out Cal. He'd dived. The bubbles from his regulator were a little too fast and hard, but he wasn't hightailing it for the surface.

She signed, "You okay?"

He nodded and signaled for an ascent.

She was *so* on board with his plan.

Ten minutes later, they were floating on the surface. Sal

wouldn't look her in the eye as he started ranting about faulty gear and a stuck valve.

"Who checked your gear?" Cal's voice was icy calm as he cut Sal off midsentence.

Sal spluttered before admitting the truth. "Piper did."

"And did she say your gear was good to go?"

"She did," Sal admitted.

"And did you adjust your gear *after* she'd given you the good-to-go?"

Sal opened his mouth. Closed it. Yep. He apparently had a pretty good idea that he'd emptied his own tank. "I wasn't getting enough air," he said defensively.

"Piper did a damned fine job." Cal's tone dared Sal to contradict him.

Sal, not being stupid, kept his mouth shut.

PIPER AND CAL dropped the Fiesta team off at their hotel. Sal took the opportunity to get in one last crack at his defective tank—Piper was certain no one but Sal believed his story—and then she headed back to Dream Big and Dive. She needed to get out of her wet gear and into something dry. She also needed a drink after today's drama, but that would have to come later.

"Are you coming in?" she asked, unlocking the door.

Cal shot her a look she couldn't interpret.

"I didn't deliberately sabotage your dive," she said in self-defense. "I don't think any of us could have predicted Sal's overreaction to a horn shark."

He took her gear bag from her and pushed the door open. "I never thought you did."

"Oh." She stepped inside and he followed, closing and locking the door behind them. "You look like someone kicked your puppy."

"Today didn't go as planned," he admitted. "You had

my back, Piper. I'd be a first-class asshole if I questioned how you did it."

She waved a hand. "Well, you do have your moments." Laughing, she danced away from him when he pretended to swat her butt. "Keep the kinky stuff to yourself."

"You did a good job," he said. "You kept Sal from drowning himself or surfacing too fast. He may be way down at the bottom of our favorite-persons list, but he's also not spending the next couple of hours in a decompression chamber."

She made a face. "Yeah. I rocked, right up until the point he snagged my regulator from me."

"He weighs two hundred pounds. You weigh—" He checked himself.

"Wise move." She grinned. "And *don't* finish your sentence."

"I wouldn't dream of it."

"And I appreciate the assist," she said more seriously. "That's the second time you've jumped in to rescue me."

"In one piece is good," he said roughly. "I like you whole, Piper."

Too bad she always came apart in his arms.

"I'm going to change," she yelled, refusing to think right now about how he made her feel. Instead, she headed into the backroom. "I'll be right back. Make yourself at home."

Part of her wanted to invite him back and try out a few late-night fantasies of hers but, really, the dive shop was both a little too public—and too uncomfortable. She was definitely a fan of mattresses. She stripped off quickly, pulling on a pink sundress and panties. Her phone rang right as she finished up—*Jaws* again—so she headed back out front as she answered.

"I've got a second offer," Del said before she could get further than hello.

"There's a surprise." Today had not gone well. "And hello to you, too."

"I need a yes or no from you."

"You promised me two weeks," she said. Cal raised an eyebrow and motioned to ask if he should step outside. The gesture was sweet, but he didn't need to go. She shook her head and made a stay gesture. "I'll hear about the Fiesta contract later this week."

"Piper—" Just once, she wanted someone to say her name without sighing or groaning in frustration. Although she might cut Cal a break. She grinned. He groaned so well.

"I'll have an answer for you soon," she promised and hung up.

"Bad news?" Given how stormy Piper's face looked right now, Cal figured he knew the answer to his question.

"Not yet." She sighed and tossed her phone into her bag. "I own only a partial interest in Dream Big and Dive. Del, my former coach, put in eighty percent of the cash, so he's calling the shots and he wants to sell."

"Ouch." Piper liked being the one in control, which he completely got. He felt the same way himself. She'd put a lot of effort into the business, as well, so having someone threaten to pull the rug out from underneath her would be a blow.

"So…when I win the Fiesta contract, I'll be able to line up financing."

"And if you don't?"

She waved a hand toward the shop. "Then Del will sell his interest to someone else. I'd rather own my own place."

"You really think he'd sell to someone else when you've expressed an interest?"

She made a face. "He already has two cash offers. I

mean, really? Who knew a used dive shop on Discovery Island would be such a hot commodity?"

Since she was looking up, she didn't catch the moment he froze because…yeah. He knew *precisely* who was bidding on her place, didn't he? Probably. He didn't know for certain, he reminded himself. Still, since it couldn't hurt to double-check, he texted Tag to look into the purchase. Surely he hadn't just tried to buy her place out from underneath her.

He'd accidentally taken one dream away from her when his motor boat had crashed into her Jet Ski, so fate must be laughing her ass off at the possibility that he was about to K.O. another dream.

"Thanks," he said as his phone vibrated.

"I owed you one." She didn't look like she was in any hurry to leave. Instead, she peered down the street. "Did you bring the Harley or the truck today?"

"Truck. Piper—"

Her fingers walked up his arm. "Someone might owe someone else a night."

"True." He leaned down and brushed a kiss over her mouth. "Is this someone interested in settling up tonight?"

"I'd never renege on a bet. Are you collecting?"

"Absolutely."

13

"MY PLACE?" HE LIKED the breathless sound of her question. Liked knowing she was as hot for him as he was for her.

"Mine." He definitely wanted to see her in his bed, her hair spread out over his pillow. If that made him some kind of atavistic Neanderthal, it didn't make the urge any less true.

She didn't protest, so he took advantage of her easy agreement to push for taking his truck. She protested but only briefly. Five minutes later, they were zipping down the coastal road toward his cottage. She'd started the ride in her own seat, but as soon as they cleared the main town, she'd scooted nearer. Her hand on his leg moved closer and closer to the danger zone. He had no idea how she expected him to drive.

"Piper." Her name came out more growl than not.

"Cal?" She tucked herself against his side, her eyes twinkling up at him. She was good at keeping him off balance, he admitted. He never knew what she'd do next, just that it would be unpredictable.

"You might want to think twice about what you're doing before I drive us off the road." He enjoyed her touch, plain and simple, but he needed to keep his mind on the road.

She made a show of looking out the window. *His* window. Piper clearly liked living dangerously, because her breasts brushed his shoulder. Twice.

"At least it would be a water landing. We could play rescue swimmer."

Right. He shook his head. And drove a little faster.

"You really want to play it safe?" she asked, when he didn't say anything.

"Five minutes. Then you can be as bad as you want."

"As *I* want?" she asked.

"Or I want," he said, knowing he was smiling.

She settled back in her seat, a grin playing over her own mouth. He had the urge to lean over and kiss it off. "You need to learn to take a few chances," she said.

The turn to his place appeared on their right, and he steered the truck down the winding driveway.

"Not right now." He threw the parking brake on and killed the engine. "Last stop."

"You probably locked your door, too," she said, ignoring him.

The action was simply prudent. Piper was waiting for him when he came around the truck, however, so all thoughts of caution flew out of his head. When her fingers walked over his hip, exploring his pocket, he knew she could feel the thick ridge of his erection.

"Got it." She produced his keys with a little flourish.

"You bet." He dropped a quick, hard kiss on her mouth and then threaded his fingers through hers, tugging her toward the door. Getting the key in the lock, he flipped it open as he kissed her again. She laughed against his mouth, the husky, warm sound flooding him with another feeling as he pulled her inside.

"I'm not sure you needed to bother locking up." She

was breathless when she pulled her mouth away from his, laughing as she surveyed his place or what there was of it. He'd opened up one wall of the kitchen in order to rewire and rip out siding that had been riddled with dry rot. As a result, his kitchen "wall" consisted of a blue plastic tarp and several yards of caution tape.

"Feel free to leave and come back in through the alternate exit," he said drily. Her answering laughter lit up her face, forming small crinkles at the corners of her eyes. She was beautiful, standing there in his house.

"I'll stay put." She gave him another smile. "Maybe next time."

His kitchen definitely wasn't winning any design awards. It still had the avocado-green appliances and the worn-out linoleum installed at least four decades ago by the original owner. Cal had decorated with stacks of paint cans, tools, and—she counted—three toolboxes. If he owned a kitchen table and chairs—or even pots, pans, anything remotely kitchenlike —she didn't see them in here.

"Kitchens are for cooking," she pointed out.

"And eating," he agreed. "Mine's a work in progress."

"I HAVE AN IDEA," he said.

"Oh?" Her rescue swimmer had a wicked look in his eyes as he prowled toward her.

"You don't seem to have the proper respect for my kitchen. I think I should rectify that."

"Did you bring me here for my opinion on your remodeling skills?" She raised an eyebrow at him.

"Not a chance," he said, and in one smooth move, he picked her up and set her on the counter. Then he stepped in, his palms on either side of her. The look in his eyes, hungry and wild, had her heart aching for him. She was proud of what he'd accomplished as a SEAL. Part of her wished she could tell him just how proud she was, but his diving issues bothered him and she was afraid he'd misinterpret her words.

"Kissing time?" Heat curled through her belly. Hooking her legs around his waist, she rested her heels on his fine butt and ran her hands up his chest.

"Absolutely."

He captured her hands and curled them around the edges of the countertop. His thumbs stroked her fingers and palms as he positioned her.

"Don't let go."

"Are we playing kinky games now?" Oh, how she hoped so.

He gave her an amused look. "You have an impressive imagination."

He placed his hands on her knees, stepping in farther until her thighs were spread apart and she felt the heat and hardness of his chest. His hands pushed gently, then stroked upward, pulling up the filmy skirt of her sundress. The adrenaline rush of diving, of *competing,* warred with Sal's accident and Cal's calm, determined rescue. Cal had been as effortlessly in control of that as he was of this moment.

Deliberately, he eased her back on the countertop, pulling her legs over his shoulders. *Definitely promising.*

Warm hands slid beneath her and cupped her butt as a wicked mouth blew gently over the center of her panties.

"Really? Right here?"

"Mmm. You accused me of never being spontaneous. I'm working on changing for you."

She forgot all about the cool counter as he tucked an old sweatshirt beneath her head. The cotton smelled like his soap and an outdoorsy, fresh scent. Please, please, please, let this be as good as she remembered. She tugged on her ear for luck.

His fingers caught hers. "You don't need luck."

"A girl can never have too much luck."

Instead of answering her, he leaned forward and kissed her, a soft, gentle pressure right on her center. His tongue traced her through the silky fabric. Once. Twice. Her breath shuddered out as she relaxed into his hold.

The next few minutes got heated. At some point, in between his kisses and her moans, he managed to remove her panties.

"Very nice," he said huskily, tucking the pink satin scrap neatly on the counter beside them. She bit back a small smile. That was her Cal.

He came back to her, and his tongue touched her. He kissed her and loved her, and he was in no rush.

Everything in her tightened, a drumbeat of *yesyesyesyes* pulsing through her body.

"You're so beautiful," he said hoarsely. She exhaled in a hard, sharp rush of air, her lower body clenching as his tongue found her again.

She could fall for a man like this. The thought stilled her, and Cal, being Cal, noticed. His head came up.

"You okay?" Concern darkened his eyes, his fingers stroking lightly over her. "Honey? You with me here?"

She was in so much trouble. This thing she had with Cal was temporary insanity. Chemistry. Whatever they called it, neither of them had called it permanent. She had no business falling in love with him.

"I'm fine." She tugged on his shoulders, bringing him right where she needed him.

"Back," she demanded.

"Bossy." The laughter was there in his voice again.

"I'm blaming you," she said. Then his mouth found

her again, and he drove her crazy, until her whimpers and moans filled the kitchen and she called out his name, pulling his head closer, harder...*more.*

A long time later, he pulled her off the counter and sat down with her right on the floor. Apparently, he really didn't have any chairs. She only hoped he had a bed. Or a mattress. *Something.* She might be desperate enough to make do with a sleeping bag. Since she was parked on his lap, she was fine, but he was the one sitting on the floor. In just a few minutes, he'd acquired a film of sawdust on his blue jeans. He hadn't been kidding about living in a construction zone.

He rested his chin on her head. "We shouldn't have done that."

He wasn't allowed to have regrets until later.

She blinked, still breathless. "Speak for yourself, but if you're worried about your technique, we can try it again in about ten minutes."

His rough chuckle had her melting all over again. "I'm suddenly feeling unexpectedly attached to these countertops."

She thought about that for a moment.

"Is there anywhere you're *done* remodeling? Just so we don't put your remodel on hiatus?"

His arms tightened around her. "Funny you should ask. The bedroom. And the bath."

"Excellent priorities." She wasn't sure she was going to be able to stir.

"Can I interest you in a change in venue?"

"Only if it doesn't involve moving," she groaned. "And if you promise you have an actual bed in there. The counter's fun, but it's hard."

"Not a problem." He scooped her up and headed down

the hallway to where she hoped and prayed he had a bedroom. With a bed. "I'll show you something else that's hard," he said with a wink.

CAL NOT ONLY had a mattress, but he had a bed frame. He'd paid a visit to one of those mattress stores with two hundred floor models, which was one hundred ninety-eight more choices than he'd needed. Hard or soft. That worked for him as far as choices went. He'd pointed, forked over a credit card and then spent more time arranging delivery to Discovery Island than he'd planned on.

It was worth every minute.

He set Piper down in the center of his bed, and she looked like she belonged. Her eyes were closed, but she was smiling. He sat down next to her.

"Better?" he asked.

"I could definitely take a nap. For which I blame you."

"Hey," he said, with mock offense. "Credit, please. I'll take the credit."

Her hum of agreement said it all. And the look on her face—sated, he decided. She looked sated. Along with tousled and pleasured. It was a good look for her. He hadn't planned on taking a nap—parts of him were definitely interested in continuing their kitchen activities—but they had the entire night in front of them and spending it wrapped around her seemed like a fine idea.

She cracked an eyelid but didn't move when the bed swayed as he stood up. He pulled his T-shirt over his head, folded it and set it on top of the chair that was almost the sum total of the furniture in the room. One bed, one chair, which doubled as a table, and his duffel bag of clothes. The only other thing he had was the Maglite he used for bedside lighting. He didn't need anything else. Bending over, he unlaced a boot.

Which apparently got her attention.

"What are you doing?" He lifted his head as he pulled off the boot and set it on the floor. She'd rolled over and the move pulled her sundress tight against her breasts.

"You said you wanted to take a nap." He shrugged. "I'm obliging you."

"Oh." She chewed on her lower lip while he worked on the second boot. "Are you always so literal?"

"Do you always say stuff you don't mean?"

His hands went to the button of his jeans and her eyes followed right along, which made him feel like king of the world. Maybe it wasn't nap time, after all. Just in case she still wasn't feeling what he was, he gave her a nice, slow show.

"Wow. I had no idea you were such a tease." Her eyes didn't move from his buttons, though, and he was lost. He had no idea how she made him feel this way, but he had a sneaking suspicion Piper had him wrapped around her fingers.

He popped buttons two and three. "Maybe I have hidden depths?"

She grinned at him. "Or maybe I could be convinced to *not* nap."

He pretended to think, letting his fingers hover over button number four. "Are you convinced?"

Button number four went the way of his predecessors, and her eyes darkened. "It's looking good," she agreed.

The fifth button was really just eye candy, he decided, but he undid it anyhow, then shoved his jeans and his boxers down.

"See anything you like?"

"Over here," she ordered, sprawling back and pointing to the patch of bed beside her. "Now."

She was definitely a bed hog. He'd noticed that before,

but chalked it up to his being in her bed. This was his bed, however, and she'd claimed two-thirds of the space. He paused just long enough to remove a condom from his wallet, before dropping his jeans back on top of the pile. Then he moved swiftly, scooping her up and making room for himself. He put the unopened condom on the chair. Not the smoothest move in the world but in the interest of being prepared, he told himself. Not because he was assuming or because he might be reduced to begging if this didn't go the way he hoped.

God, he was hoping.

"You're overlooking one thing," he said.

"Oh?" She linked her arms around his neck. They were close enough now for him to rest his forehead on hers, to brush his mouth over her cheek. He did both while she tried to formulate her question. He was getting to her, he thought, fiercely glad. "What's that?"

"This is my night. I give the orders," he growled.

And there it was…the heated curiosity he loved about her. "Don't let me stop you," she answered and, yep, her words were pure command.

"I can see this is going to be hard for you." He pressed into her and she laughed. He loved her laugh. The sound reminded him of margaritas on the beach, sweet but with a wicked kick, the strawberry and salt on the cool glass leaving a warm burn in his belly. Maybe they could try this again in Mexico sometime. If things worked out with Fiesta, and she was still talking to him after learning he'd bought her dive shop.

She stretched up into him, tugging him down.

"You're wearing far too many clothes, if we're not napping," he pointed out.

Lifting up, he reached for the hem of her dress. She helped with another one of those crazy-making wriggles.

Her dress went up, catching on her shoulders, and she was completely, beautifully bare. No panties. He almost came on the spot.

"We forgot your panties in the kitchen," he whispered roughly.

"Who's this we, kemosabe?" She tugged the dress free and tossed it over the side of the bed. Her skin was bronzed from her time outdoors except for the white lines from her swimsuit. He traced the mark on her shoulder with his fingers, following the path downward until he cupped her breast with his hand. Her breathing sped up.

"So, no nap?" She curled a leg around his waist, rocking against him.

"Not for at least an hour." His mouth needed to follow his fingers, he decided, starting with her shoulder and then going lower. When his tongue discovered her nipple, she groaned.

"Is that all you've got in you? An hour?" She was laughing at him. An answering grin spread across his face. He blew lightly on her nipple, and her heel dug into his back. He cupped her other breast with his free hand. Equal time sounded right to him.

"I'd be happy to keep you up all night and most of tomorrow."

"Promises," she said happily.

Since he had all the time in the world, he explored her breasts leisurely, kissing and licking them. Sucking the tips gently into his mouth. When he caught one hard tip carefully between his teeth and pressed, she arched up off the bed.

"Cal."

He shifted up so he could kiss her as he moved his hands lower at the same time. There were definite advantages to forgetting her panties in his kitchen. Her hands were also as busy as his mouth. She reached between his legs and palmed his erection, and just like that, his universe narrowed to one woman with wicked hands. She stroked him from base to tip, squeezing gently.

He covered her mouth with his, kissing her hard and deep. She opened up for him, her tongue tangling up with his. Two mouths, two tongues, but he had no idea where he ended or she began. The poetic crap he'd heard before suddenly made a whole new world of sense. He could feel his body blending into hers, and guess what? It was good. *Better* than good.

So he kissed her and enjoyed every second of it. The rough, little sounds she was making—sexy whimpers and throaty gasps because Piper had always, always been happy to *tell* him what she wanted—said she was enjoying this, too. That she was right there with him.

Without breaking their marathon kiss, he pressed a finger into her slick folds. Up, then down, swirling his fingers slowly around her clit in ever smaller circles. He loved touching her there. When he slid a finger inside, she was hot perfection. She clenched around him, and he added a second finger.

She tore her mouth away from his.

"Now," she demanded.

"My night," he reminded her. "My rules."

"Maybe you could make an exception?" She moved, and holy hotness, now the tip of him pressed against the opening of her, and he was fairly certain he couldn't remember his name, let alone the rules of the game they were playing.

He did, however, remember just enough to reach over to snag the condom from the chair and tear it open with his teeth—grateful for preparation because making the return trip across the room would have killed him—and roll the latex down before sinking deep inside her. He made a rough sound, she hummed something back and then he had her pinned flat beneath him, the bed slamming into the wall because there was no holding back now, just him and Piper.

She looked beautiful spread out beneath him. There was no better sight. Just his woman, her arms open for him. Her face turned up toward his, so close there was almost no space at all between them. She made a sexy little noise as he drew back, her breath teasing his damp skin. Her nails bit into his shoulders as she hung on, a tiny, welcome sting of pain promising she was sure right there with him.

She moaned his name.

"Right here, baby," he said roughly as her hands stopped grabbing his shoulders and cupped the sides of his face instead to draw him down for another heated kiss. That worked for him. Her tongue pushed into his mouth, mimicking his rhythm as he drove into her. Sexy. Hot as hell. She was all that—*more* than that—and he wanted to tell her how she made him feel, but no way was he letting go of her. So, instead, he kissed her some more because tonight he was all about the show-and-tell.

She felt so incredible, all liquid heat, her inner muscles squeezing him as she got closer. Being close with Piper was something else again. He wasn't sure what the something was, but twice wasn't going to be enough. He could do this over and over for the next fifty years or so.

Since he had only tonight, however, he'd make the most of every second. He pulled back and then sank into her again, deeper this time. Did it again. Piper's body pulled at him, trying to hold on to him, as though that part of her was in full agreement with his over-and-over-for-half-of-forever sentiment. He could feel the sharp pulses as she got nearer, and he reached a hand between them, happy to give her what she wanted.

He braced his other hand against the pillow beside her head, loving the way her hair spilled over his fingers, her face close enough to touch. She smelled like green apples and soap, Piper and woman, a sweet, sexy scent with an edge that drove him crazy. Her skin was soft everywhere he touched, but beneath the softness was muscled strength. She'd worked herself back from her injury, and her body reflected the way she drove herself through life. She didn't hold back, going all out for her goal.

She moved against him as he drove in and out of her, his hips meeting hers in a primitive closeness. Faster. *Harder.* Her body gripped his, squeezing him firmly, as his fingers plucked her tight, needy clit with each thrust.

"Cal." His name was a raw moan, all feminine demand on her lips.

"I'm here," he promised and gave her what they both wanted, slamming his hips against hers, driving himself deeper, quicker. He couldn't hold on much longer, but he needed her to come for him. *With* him. He cupped her face, capturing her mouth in a kiss that was raw and urgent, watching her face as she climaxed because he loved seeing her come undone. As soon as she went over the edge, he let go himself, pumping himself hard and fast into her as she held him tight.

14

SHE'D TOLD HERSELF that winning wasn't everything (okay, so Piper might have been kidding herself just a little there). Without the Fiesta contract, she had no hope of securing the bank financing, and Del would sell his half of the dive business. At best, she'd have a new partner who might let her continue to run things the way she had. At worst, she'd have a fight on her hands. It was hard to concentrate, though, when she would have rather been replaying yesterday's memories of Cal. He'd kept her up most of the night, and it had been worth it.

When her cell phone rang, her heart leaped. Fiesta had finally come a-calling.

"Victory is ringing." Carla nudged the phone toward her. "Answer it."

Right.

She'd have her answer in four, three, two… She hesitated. It would be over. She and Cal would settle their bet, play out their remaining nights and then go back to… whatever it was they were before. Friendly competitors. Neighbors.

"If Fiesta hangs up, I'll kill you," Carla said conversationally.

Piper picked up the phone and tapped the talk button.

"Piper Clark speaking." Her voice sounded sure and confident, and Fate had to be on her side, because none of the nauseating churn in her stomach came through in her voice.

Sal Britten answered, darn it. Maybe Fate wasn't in such a good mood, after all.

"This is a difficult call to make," Sal said and his self-satisfied voice made her question her decision not to let him drown. Okay. Not really, but letting him flounder for just a few more seconds might have improved his personality.

And then she processed his words and mouthed a really foul obscenity. Any conversation beginning with those four words didn't come with a happy ending.

Sal, however, was perfectly happy. He kept right on talking, not pausing for breath. "While we at Fiesta Cruise Lines were extremely impressed with your proposal, Piper, we've decided to go in another direction."

Carla looked at her expectantly.

"I see, *Sal.*" She hadn't missed his deliberate use of her first name. He was a patronizing asshole. And then she processed his words. "Dream Big and Dive has not been awarded the contract."

Carla thumped her head down on the counter. Piper pretty much felt the same way, but it was like a diving competition where you'd been matching the leader on the scoreboard point for point and then, when the final scores flashed up on the board, you realized that some itty-bitty percentage of a point had gone to the other diver, who would get to stand on the podium instead of you. It sucked, but you put your game face on and congratulated the winner. Took a few photos on the sidelines, waved and beat the fastest, most graceful retreat possible to the locker room, because once you were in the shower, you had plausible deniability for the tears.

"We're awarding the contract to Deep Dive," Sal continued, oblivious to the way her world was imploding around her.

Of course. Cal would be a gracious winner. He always was. "May I ask why?" she gritted out.

Sal being Sal, he was delighted to pontificate further. "His performance on our last dive sealed the deal."

Right. The dive Sal had screwed up so badly they had had to rescue his drowning ass. Apparently, her part in that whole save-his-butt endeavor either hadn't made much of an impression or hadn't made it back to the Fiesta board. Frankly, she was surprised Sal had brought it up at all.

"We extended the offer to him earlier today and he accepted."

Even better. She was the insurance in case for some reason Cal turned down their offer. Fiesta hadn't wanted to give her the blow-off speech until they'd been sure of him.

She didn't do tears, she reminded herself. Crying wouldn't help.

A dive slate appeared in her field of vision. "BRB," Carla had scrawled. She nodded her head as she processed the shorthand for "be right back" and tried to concentrate on the blah blah blah coming her way from Sal. Since she was clearly not hired, she figured she was entitled to honesty.

"His rescue sealed the deal?"

"He was very impressive."

Piper made a mental note to tell Cal that one.

"And you're expecting near drowning to be a common occurrence on your Fiesta-sponsored dives, and therefore you had to go with a professional rescue swimmer?" she asked sweetly.

The dead silence on the other end was her answer. Sal

was undoubtedly calculating how fast he could hang up on her now that he'd delivered his bad news.

"Thank you for *your* time," she said and ended the call. Since Fiesta wasn't going to be paying her, she didn't have to put up with Sal anymore. That was one silver lining.

But…wow. She ran through the details of her proposal in her head, mentally walking through the demo dive. She'd been so sure the Fiesta team had loved her dive, that they'd understood exactly how much fun a shipload of cruisers and newbie divers could have swimming with the sea lions. And, instead, she'd been trumped when Mr. Heroic Navy Swimmer had come charging to the rescue.

Worse, if she hadn't offered to lead Cal's dive, none of this would have happened. He would have got into the water or not—she was betting strongly on the *not*—but he wouldn't have taken over for her. She thought about it for a moment. She'd had his back. Had covered for him. And it had backfired on her, hadn't it?

Carla came back inside the shop, carrying a cardboard tray with paper coffee cups. She flipped the open sign to closed and locked the door. The gesture was appreciated, but caffeine wasn't the Band-Aid Piper needed right now.

"Never forget who the competition is," she told Carla.

"Got it." Carla popped a cup free and handed it over.

"I rescue Cal's butt and therefore he won." Saying it out loud wasn't as therapeutic as she'd anticipated.

Carla took a sip from her own cup. "At least he's got a mighty fine butt."

"Irrelevant."

"Would you feel better about losing to him if he wasn't a hottie?"

Would she? "No."

Carla motioned toward the cup. "Drink. It'll make you feel better."

"I'm not in the mood for coffee."

"Good thing I didn't bring you coffee."

Piper took a cautious sip. With Carla, anything was possible. Sure enough, sweet and salty, the margarita froze her teeth and hit her stomach like a rock.

"Where did you find margaritas at—" she checked her phone "—ten in the morning?"

"Big Petey's. He likes you."

And she definitely liked his margaritas. Mainlining her weight in the sweet stuff was unexpectedly appealing, but it wouldn't erase her loss. The Fiesta contract had gone to Cal.

"So," Carla said. "Next steps?"

"I've got an appointment with the loan officer tomorrow over on the mainland."

Carla nodded. "And you're keeping it?"

"Yes." She had no idea how she'd convince the guy to take a chance on her and shower her business with cash, but she'd figure something out. "He had 'questions about my cash flow,'" she said, making air quotes. "The Fiesta contract was the perfect answer to those questions."

"Rest in peace, dear dream of a partner buyout." Carla raised her coffee cup. "What about your bet?"

Wow. *That* had completely slipped her mind. She now owed Cal one night of yes-master-what-can-I-do-for-you-master sex. Or at least that was what she'd imagined—with the roles reversed—when she'd made the stupid bet in the first place.

"Your face is flushed," Carla observed. "I'm going to assume you're not worried about paying up."

Nope. That would be a resounding *look forward to it.*

PIPER WAS OUTSIDE her dive shop, locking up, when Cal drove up on his Harley. He had to be the last person she wanted to see right now, so he had no idea why he'd come looking for her. He hadn't come to gloat or rub her face in it or even to tease, although he doubted she'd see it that way. He'd gotten the call, accepted the congratulations, and yet the whole time, he'd been thinking about Piper. While he was printing out the Fiesta contract and pretending to read the fine print (until Tag had taken the pages from him), he'd imagined Piper getting her call. Someone would be telling her that she'd lost and Cal had won.

With the new revenue, he'd be able to hire more former SEALs. He knew plenty of good guys who were struggling to find the right place for themselves after leaving the service, and Deep Dive could fill that need. He still had plenty of work to do on his own head, but with the Fiesta contract he could give other veterans the same opportunity. He'd listened to Daeg and Tag making celebratory plans but hadn't been able to drum up any enthusiasm.

He had what he wanted, except…suddenly it wasn't enough. It wasn't what mattered *most*. Piper was.

So he'd headed over here.

Like an idiot.

He killed the engine on the Harley and coasted toward the sidewalk. She had her back to him, so there was the small possibility she hadn't heard him coming. Faded blue jeans cupped her butt and ended just above a pair of kickass boots. The dive shop T-shirt she wore hugged her breasts and she had a messenger bag slung over her chest. She didn't look angry, but then again, she hadn't seen him yet. She turned around, reaching up to pull her hair into a ponytail. The move emphasized the way her shirt clung to some of his favorite places. When she saw him, her face froze.

"You heard the news." *Stupid,* he chided himself.

"Congratulations." She didn't move, just stood there

and looked at him. The three feet of space between them suddenly felt like three million miles.

"Piper—"

She walked toward him. For a moment, he thought she was coming to him, and he wasn't ashamed to admit he was fiercely glad. Maybe winning didn't have to mess things up. Maybe she could accept this and even his partial ownership of her dive shop. Then, of course, she brushed past him and straddled her bike. She was leaving.

"I'm going to follow you," he warned. She didn't get to run from this.

"I don't want to talk right now." She fished in her bag for her keys.

He didn't want to talk, either, not if he was honest. He wanted to share his good news with her and hold her because the news hadn't been good for her. Those two things were incompatible, however, and he had no idea how to solve things for her.

"I thought about dropping out," he admitted.

She grabbed her helmet from the back of her seat. "I didn't. I'm a big girl, Cal. I don't need you to hand me things. Or fix them. I lost and I'll handle it."

The look in her eyes was part pride, part sadness and humor. "Tell me you're okay."

"I'm fine." She flashed him a quick smile. "I may not *like* losing, but I do know how to do it. Next time, however, I'm going to kick your butt. Consider yourself warned."

Next time sounded good to him.

She pulled the helmet on, started the Harley and pushed away from the curb. Definitely leaving. He opened his mouth to say something, although he had no idea what, and then she looked back at him.

"Are you coming? Or are you afraid I'm going to kill

you and hide the body so I can get my hands on that contract?"

He could feel a stupid grin tugging at his mouth. "I'm not afraid."

"Nope?" She moved down the street, and he steered his bike beside hers.

"You bet," he said, raising his voice to be heard over the engine. "The only thing I'm afraid of is that you *won't* put your hands on me."

"Your place," she suggested and took off. And, even though she went twenty miles over the speed limit, he was right behind her.

THE FIRST TIME was fast and hard. Piper blamed that on the adrenaline rush of racing Cal. Not the most responsible thing she'd ever done, but she deserved some fun today. The strip of road hugging the island's coast was deserted, and she hadn't gone over fifty. Much. She'd tried to race him into the house, too, but he'd beaten her to the door. Of course, it was his front door and, Cal being Cal, he'd undoubtedly locked it, but it was the principle of the matter. She'd gotten there first.

"Got you," he'd announced in a thrillingly rough voice, slapping his hands down on either side of her head. Cal in a playful mood was both new and sexy, so she hadn't protested at all when he'd swept her off her feet, opened the door and carried her down the hall to the bedroom. Instead, she'd suggested a second race, to see who could strip down the fastest. She'd won *that* one.

The sun was setting now, painting fiery strips of orange and red over the ocean's surface. She didn't want to move. He'd worn her out, but not before she'd put one hell of a smile on his face.

"Was that four—or five?" His smoky, gruff voice rumbled in her ear and she squirmed. She'd be happy to up his count.

She pretended to think. "I had at least five. It's not my fault if you got beat."

"I'm a guy." His hand cupped the back of her neck, his thumb rubbing a small circle against her skin. He'd done the same thing elsewhere, and her body hummed just thinking about it. Cal had magic hands. "We don't recover as fast."

She could hear the smile in his voice. "Again, not my problem."

"You're a tough woman." He dropped a kiss on her head and she snuggled in closer.

"I am glad for you." It had to be said, and somehow it was easier like this. The room was getting darker now as the sun slipped down behind the horizon. Even without lifting her head, she could just make out the clothing scattered everywhere, along with most of the pillows from the bed. They'd made a mess.

He shifted, tugging her up until he could see her face. Of course, the position also meant she could see his, which was no hardship.

"Good," he said roughly. "I don't want you to be unhappy."

She stared at his familiar face. What did he want? Had he thought about where they went from here? He was supposed to be a chemistry problem she worked through, not a permanent fixture in her life. And yet…she couldn't help wondering what-if.

"I need to tell you something," he said.

And…cue the bad news.

"You're married. You're shipping out. You don't *do* relationships."

He bit out a curse.

"Now you owe me a quarter."

"What kind of guy do you think I am?"

She shrugged and rolled off him. "I don't really know you, Cal."

"Tell me what you want to know."

"Give me the bad news," she countered.

He scrubbed a hand over his head. "Del is selling his half of your dive business. I made an offer. We're going to be partners, you and I."

Over her dead body. Or his. Yeah. She liked the sound of that. "How long have you known?"

"Del accepted my offer right after the Fiesta dive."

No way. "You're joking. Please tell me you're joking."

"You don't like the idea." He didn't sound surprised— more resigned.

"Cal." She stared at him. "The only place we don't fight is in bed."

"You can't have it all," she said, jumping out of bed. "You should have told me."

"Piper—" He didn't know what to say.

"I'm done here."

"You can't just walk out on us," he said. "I want this to work."

"I like the sound of that." And she did. Too much.

"I hear a but."

Score one for him. "But you knew I wanted to own Dream Big and Dive. I told you that, and yet you went ahead and bought Del's half of the business anyhow."

He sat up in bed, the sheet falling back to his waist. Part of her wanted to push him down and lose herself in the way he made her feel. The rest of her, however, knew that at some point the hot sex would come to an end and they'd have to work together. Live together. The sex wasn't enough because somewhere along the line, he'd made her want all of him.

"Del was going to sell anyhow," he pointed out. She hated how calm and logical he sounded. "Aren't I better than a random stranger?"

"I don't know how I feel about that. You didn't ask me."

"I'm asking now," he said, his voice tight.

"After you bought in. It doesn't count."

"Make it count."

He wasn't the person who got to be angry here. He'd won the contract. He'd bought her business. In fact, he'd had everything go his way and she had not. She wasn't going to whine about it, but she *was* going to do something about it. She got out of bed and started pulling on her clothes.

"Where are you going?"

"I'm leaving." Take that. "Don't worry. I'll lock the door on the way out. Or not." She shrugged and headed for the door. "I'm not the one who worries about thieves and evil villains."

"Piper." Her name was a growl. Sheets rustled, and his feet hit the floor with a thump. Screw being dignified. She picked up her pace. She was done here.

15

It took the rest of the morning for Cal to do the math. He'd done some swimming, followed by some thinking. Then more swimming. He had the contract all to himself, and his hands were going to be plenty full as he brought more former SEALs on board—but his place felt empty without her. Hell, *he* felt empty. Piper had filled a void he didn't realize he had.

When he gave in and went looking for her, Piper wasn't at home, nor was she at the dive shop. Carla, however, was, scrolling through pictures on her phone of their last dive.

He didn't waste time with preliminaries. "Where is she?"

"Where is who?"

He wasn't buying her sweet, innocent look.

"Your boss? The woman who signs your paychecks?"

"Funny," she said, "I'd heard you were my new boss now."

"Would that make you take orders from me?" A man could hope.

"Nope," she answered, shooting him a saccharine smile. "Not in this lifetime."

"You don't want to know what I want with her?"

She shook her head. "The only thing that matters to me is what *she* wants with *you*."

"I can work with that."

"Are you going to chase after her and admit you screwed this all up?"

"I'm not apologizing for winning the Fiesta contract." Never. Maybe?

Carla made a give-it-up gesture.

"But I should have told her about my offer to buy out Del's share as soon as I realized what had happened," he admitted.

"Because?" she prompted.

"What is this, therapy hour?"

"Do you need it to be? You are a guy." She eyed him appraisingly.

He had no idea what that meant. "And?"

"You need to tell her how you feel." She held up a finger when he opened his mouth. "I'm sure you believe your reasons for buying out Del are the best, but think about it from Piper's perspective."

"You feel very secure in your job," he announced.

Carla beamed. "Piper and I go way back."

He eyed her. This was Carla, after all. Good to know Piper had someone at her back, but nothing about Carla made this easy. Or quick. "I'd like to *hear* her perspective. I'd also like to tell her a few things. Ask a question or two." He paused, then went for gold. "Please?"

"She's taking the ferry over to the mainland."

"She's leaving?"

He turned and headed for the door.

"The ferry leaves in fifteen minutes," she called after him. "You can fire me after you get her back."

Yep. That was definitely gloating he heard in her voice.

16

Cal broke every traffic law on his way down to the ferry dock. The side streets weren't made for speed, but he pushed eighty on the Harley. If he laid down his bike, he wouldn't get there in time, but he couldn't bring himself to ease up. *Piper* was at stake here. He tried to imagine staying on Discovery Island without her, and it wasn't a pretty picture. He had no idea how it had happened, but he'd fallen for Piper Clark.

Ten blocks. Two traffic lights, six stop signs and two four-way stops. And then he had the ferry dock in his sights. The heavy boat rode low in the water, loaded up with cars. He was close enough now to make out the tourists on the upper decks, chatting and laughing as they snapped their final photos of Discovery Island. The ramp was still down and he breathed a sigh of relief. He wasn't completely out of time. He parked the Harley in a no-parking zone, so sue him—and vaulted over the turnstile.

"I'm not riding," he hollered at Mary Beth, the woman working the ticket booth as he sprinted toward her. "I need to talk to Piper and then I'll be back."

He'd known Mary Beth forever. The older woman and his mother were friends and members in the Red Hat Society. Some of their antics scared the piss out of him. A spur-of-the-moment cruise to Cabo with tattoos came to mind. Since Mary Beth and his mother talked, she probably already knew his business anyhow, and could cut him some slack.

She flashed a thumbs-up as he barreled past and indeed seemed disinclined to call for security.

"Ten minutes," she hollered after him. "That's all you've got."

He'd make ten minutes be enough time.

He sprinted onto the ferry, heart banging against his ribs. The ferry had two levels, plus the car hold. It also had a gift shop and a snack shop, in addition to all the off-limits, personnel-only areas. Think, he told himself. If you were Piper, where would you be?

The answer was immediate and obvious. She'd be up front where the riders felt the chop and half of them ended up drenched from the spray. Unfortunately, she wasn't the only daredevil riding the ferry today, and there were too many people to run, so he strode forward, bellowing her name. Heads turned as he worked his way out onto the forward deck. Yeah. He'd apparently left his pride at the dive shop. Again, this was Piper at stake. He was pretty much sure he'd do anything for her.

And...bingo.

Piper stood at the very front of the ferry, fingers wrapped around the guardrail. Thank God—he had an immediate flashback to the summer she'd decided to reenact the *Titanic* and pretended to be the woman on the masthead. Then, she'd stood on the railings—*on the outside*—her arms flung wide, hair blowing in the breeze. It had been a testament to her sense of balance and the existence of guardian angels that she hadn't toppled off and been sucked under the ferry.

She was wearing the business-casual number she'd worn to her Fiesta presentation and the short white dress drove him just as crazy today as it had then. She also had her earbuds in, so once again, she hadn't heard him bellowing her name. That was apparently going to be a pattern in their relationship. He'd deal with it. He moved up behind her, wrapped an arm around her waist and tugged the earbuds free.

"Your music's too loud." Shit. That wasn't what he'd meant to say at all.

She looked surprised to see him, which didn't bode well. Then she glared down at his arm. "Let go."

The ferry gave a deafening warning blast of its horn, and the pace picked up twenty feet away, down on the dock. Fewer than ten minutes until departure. He had no idea how to explain.

"Cal?"

"Stay." Okay, so his words had come out more order than request. Old habits died hard and she'd probably make him work on his delivery. *If* he could convince her to stay.

"Excuse me?" Her head snapped up, her mouth opening in shock. Yeah. He definitely needed to work on his delivery.

"With me, Piper. Stay with me. Don't go."

She shook her head. "That's…" She inhaled deeply, her fingers tightening on the railing. "I'm not even sure where to start."

"Stay with me," he repeated. Jesus. He had what, nine minutes? He should have prepared a speech. Run through some words in his head instead of hopping on his bike and driving like a man mad.

"For how long, Cal? How well do you think we'd work together at Dream Big and Dive? You won. I lost."

"This isn't about winning or losing." He moved forward,

trapping her between his body and the railing. When she wriggled furiously, he wrapped a leg around hers. The move wasn't nice, but he had only eight minutes.

"The he-man routine isn't working for me," she warned.

"I'll adjust," he offered.

"Right." She wriggled again, and he was pretty certain there would be at least a dozen pictures of them on Facebook within the hour.

Her gaze roamed over his face, searching for something. He needed words, directions...a clue. Instead, he got nothing.

"I want a second chance," he said. "I want you to believe me on this."

CAL WRAPPED HIS arms tight around her as he took shameless advantage of being bigger and stronger. She wriggled one more time, just to make the point that she was a strong, independent woman, and then she let herself relax against him. He felt so good, solid and warm, and apparently her inner wild child liked being manhandled—just a little—because she suddenly had a whole lot less interest in being on time for her appointment with the bank officer.

"A second chance at what?" she asked.

His sigh fanned her hair.

"Everything, Piper."

"You're going to have to be more specific."

They'd kissed. They'd made love—okay, it turned out *she'd* made love and maybe he'd been more in it for the hot sex—and they'd looked out for each other. That wasn't really a long-term relationship. Cal wasn't offering her a solid reason to *stay*. He might say he wanted a second chance at them, but she didn't know whether he meant at the dive shop—or her heart.

"I need to go," she said quietly.

He looked down at her. "Is that really what you want?"

She'd spent her whole life competing, in it to win it. She'd always gone all out, because coming in second didn't count. It had always been about making it to the podium. About being, not just good enough, but the very best. She'd taken chances to get to that point, chances that sometimes paid off and sometimes ended in disaster. It was the nature of the game. Cal was a fighter, too, but he'd fought for people. She'd fought for herself. That didn't make her like herself very much right now. Worse, her heart broke at the thought of Cal walking away from her. What if having temporarily had him was worse than not having had him at all?

"I think there's a good chance we're good at fighting— and at *chemistry,*" she said carefully. His mouth quirked, the familiar gesture making her want to stay in his arms forever. "But you're the one who keeps telling me not to take chances, Cal. To look before I leap."

This time, when she twisted, he let her go. The ferry blew its last warning blast, the engines revving and churning up the water. The gangway rattled as it was withdrawn.

"You're going to miss your exit," she warned.

"I was wrong," he said, not moving.

That made two of them. She didn't want to compete with him, as fun as that had been. She wanted to compete *for* him, but that was a game where she didn't know the rules or even if he wanted her entry.

"I love you," he said. "And I think you should take a chance on us, because I'm sure going to."

She took a step back and watched him. Instead of heading for the exit, he turned and walked over to the railing. The ferry lurched forward, moving slowly away from the dock.

"I'm hoping you might consider loving me back."

His words hung in the air between them.

"Cal—"

"Jump with me?" he asked and held out a hand. "Take a chance. Be a daredevil. Do it because you can." His mouth curved. "Because I *dare* you. And because I'm still scared shitless of going under, but I'll take that chance with you."

Wow. He had her there. Cal never took unnecessary risks. Never jumped without an action plan and a good reason. Not sure what to say, she walked over to him and stared over the side. The ferry was still moving slowly. Only a hundred yards to shore, she decided. Or possibly two hundred, if they aimed for the beach instead of the dock. They'd both made far longer swims.

She looked at him. He waited, watching.

"You think we'd get pulled under the ferry? No. Don't answer."

He grinned instead, and her heart pounded, a sweet, warm sensation spreading everywhere inside her. Honestly, she'd take her chances on surviving the jump with the right partner. With *Cal*. She toed off her shoes and picked them up.

Half the ferry's passengers appeared to be staring at them—and she was fairly certain the ferry might, just possibly, be slowing down. Those were good odds.

"Ready?" he asked, eyeing her shoes.

"You bet."

Together they clambered over the side. Her dress presented an unexpected challenge, but screw it. If she was really planning on jumping off a ferry, flashing a few innocent bystanders was the least of her worries. Cal steadied her anyhow, as she swung her legs over.

Cal glanced down. "I must be crazy," he muttered.

"Crazy for me." She laughed and tugged on her ear. Just

once, because old habits died hard and she wanted only good things for her and Cal.

"One hundred percent. On the count of three?"

She nodded. "One. Two. Thr—"

Before she could finish, he scooped her up in his arms and jumped. She shrieked, her shoes flying free and heading out to sea independently of her. His arms tightened as they achieved a spectacular amount of air and then ripped through the surface in a cannonball of a landing.

They broke apart underwater and she kicked for the surface. When she broke it, Cal was already there, waiting for her. The ferry moved slowly away, the cheer from their audience fading slowly over the water.

"My car's leaving without me," she observed, treading water.

"It'll come back."

"And you owe me a pair of shoes."

His wet T-shirt clung to him like a second skin. She looked down and, wow, she wasn't getting out of the water until dark. Her white dress was completely see-through, plastered to the lacy pink straps of her bra. She was also clearly cold. Big deal. She turned to him.

"But you definitely got my attention."

"Good." He smiled at her, pulling her into his arms.

"Although there were probably *drier* ways to accomplish this," she said. "Do you want to tell me what that was really about?

"You were leaving," he said.

"For a business meeting at a bank, to see about possible financing. I was going to come back and kick your butt or buy it out."

His eyes closed briefly. "Then, I may have jumped the gun. Slightly."

"Oh." She wrapped her legs around his waist and let

him do the heavy lifting of keeping them afloat. "Are you taking it all back?"

"Carla left me with the impression you were moving off the island, lock, stock and barrel."

That was definitely something Carla would do. "You want to be careful around her. She's tricky."

"I realize that now." He pulled her closer still. "And you can still do it—kick my butt, find alternate funding. Whatever it takes to make you happy. Although I'd rather interest you in doing something else. I love you," he said and she wanted to hold the moment close, but he was still talking, because apparently when Cal opened up and found the words to describe what he was feeling, he didn't *stop*. "It's not just about keeping you safe or about winning and losing. I want it all—the love and the risks. The question is—will you take a chance on me? And possibly," he groaned, "take pity on me and tell me how you're feeling right now?"

She reached up and brushed her mouth over his. "I can do that. I love you."

His slow smile grew. "Good, because I'm fairly certain you owe me another night since you *lost* the Fiesta contract, and I was planning on collecting."

The tender look was back in his eyes, so she momentarily put her new plan of drowning him and swimming back to shore on hold.

"Or four or four hundred," she agreed.

"I'd be willing to compromise on *forever*."

"Deal," she said and kissed him.

* * * * *

Look for Anne Marsh's WICKED SECRETS, coming soon from Harlequin Blaze!

COMING NEXT MONTH FROM

HARLEQUIN

Blaze

Available October 21, 2014

#819 CHRISTMAS WITH A SEAL
Uniformly Hot!
by Tawny Weber
Lieutenant Phillip Banks is home for the holidays—and
Frankie Silvera is on a mission to seduce the serious but
sexy SEAL. Can he resist her arsenal of holiday cookies,
mistletoe and racy red lingerie? Not a chance!

#820 OH, NAUGHTY NIGHT!
by Leslie Kelly
Lulu Vandenburg decides to end her dating dry spell in one
naughty, uninhibited night with a sexy stranger. But the man
she chooses turns out to be someone she knows all too well....

#821 THE MIGHTY QUINNS: RYAN
The Mighty Quinns
by Kate Hoffmann
Adventure guide Ryan Quinn's job was easy: escort
übercelebrity Serena Hightower and her bridesmaids around
Fiji. But when he and Serena discover a sizzling chemistry,
they'll risk everything for the most thrilling adventure yet!

#822 IN TOO CLOSE
Holiday Heat
by Katherine Garbera
Five years ago Elizabeth Anders agreed to become
Bradley Hunt's lover if they were single at thirty. But what will
happen when these best friends finally give in to temptation?

**YOU CAN FIND MORE INFORMATION ON UPCOMING HARLEQUIN® TITLES,
FREE EXCERPTS AND MORE AT WWW.HARLEQUIN.COM.**

HBCNM1014

REQUEST YOUR FREE BOOKS!
2 FREE NOVELS PLUS 2 FREE GIFTS!

HARLEQUIN *Blaze*®

red-hot reads!

YES! Please send me 2 FREE Harlequin® Blaze™ novels and my 2 FREE gifts (gifts are worth about $10). After receiving them, if I don't wish to receive any more books, I can return the shipping statement marked "cancel." If I don't cancel, I will receive 4 brand-new novels every month and be billed just $4.74 per book in the U.S. or $4.96 per book in Canada. That's a savings of at least 14% off the cover price. It's quite a bargain. Shipping and handling is just 50¢ per book in the U.S. and 75¢ per book in Canada.* I understand that accepting the 2 free books and gifts places me under no obligation to buy anything. I can always return a shipment and cancel at any time. Even if I never buy another book, the two free books and gifts are mine to keep forever.

150/350 HDN F4WC

Name _____ (PLEASE PRINT) _____

Address _____ Apt. # _____

City _____ State/Prov. _____ Zip/Postal Code

Signature (if under 18, a parent or guardian must sign)

Mail to the **Harlequin® Reader Service:**
IN U.S.A.: P.O. Box 1867, Buffalo, NY 14240-1867
IN CANADA: P.O. Box 609, Fort Erie, Ontario L2A 5X3

Want to try two free books from another line?
Call 1-800-873-8635 or visit www.ReaderService.com.

* Terms and prices subject to change without notice. Prices do not include applicable taxes. Sales tax applicable in N.Y. Canadian residents will be charged applicable taxes. Offer not valid in Quebec. This offer is limited to one order per household. Not valid for current subscribers to Harlequin Blaze books. All orders subject to credit approval. Credit or debit balances in a customer's account(s) may be offset by any other outstanding balance owed by or to the customer. Please allow 4 to 6 weeks for delivery. Offer available while quantities last.

Your Privacy—The Harlequin® Reader Service is committed to protecting your privacy. Our Privacy Policy is available online at www.ReaderService.com or upon request from the Harlequin Reader Service.

We make a portion of our mailing list available to reputable third parties that offer products we believe may interest you. If you prefer that we not exchange your name with third parties, or if you wish to clarify or modify your communication preferences, please visit us at www.ReaderService.com/consumerschoice or write to us at Harlequin Reader Service Preference Service, P.O. Box 9062, Buffalo, NY 14269. Include your complete name and address.

HB13R2

New York Times bestselling author
Tawny Weber delivers a sexy new SEAL story.
Here's a sneak peek at

Christmas with a SEAL

The Las Vegas penthouse was a kaleidoscope of sensations. Neon lights glinted off sparkling chandeliers, sending colorful sparkles off the crowd of partiers. Dressed in everything from sequins to plastic, denim to silk, bodies filled the room, covering the leather couches, perching on chrome stools around the bar and flowing onto the dance floor.

Accenting it all were intense music, free-flowing drinks and men. So, so many men.

And, oh, baby, they were gorgeous.

It wasn't just knowing that most of these muscular, sexy men were navy SEALs that made Frankie Silvera's insides dance. It was knowing that somewhere among them was her dream hottie and the answer to all of her problems.

She just had to find him.

"See anything you like?" Lara asked, stepping up beside her.

A room full of sexy guys with smoking-hot bodies?

What wasn't to like?

"I'm here to celebrate your wedding," Frankie said. "Not to hook up."

HBEXP79823

"You're in Las Vegas, Frankie. Go wild. Have fun." Lara laughed as she turned to leave. "Don't forget, what happens in Vegas stays in Vegas."

"Tempting, but I'm not the wild Vegas type," Frankie demurred, keeping her secret dream just that—secret. Frankie wasn't about to share her hope of finding a guy she'd only seen infrequently over the past ten years and seducing him.

Especially not when the guy was Lara's brother.

Taking a second glass of liquid courage that tasted like champagne, she decided it was time to get to work on the best weekend of her life.

Not an easy task. She looked around. There were at least two hundred people here. Figuring it was a gift that all the guys were hot and sexy and made searching fun, she moved through the bodies to cross the room.

Whoa. Frankie narrowed her eyes.

Was that him?

Sitting alone in one booth and looking as if he wanted to be anywhere else, the man was nursing a drink. Mahogany hair, shorn with military precision. A navy blue sweater covered his broad shoulders, emphasizing his perfect posture and, from what she could see, a gorgeous chest.

Lieutenant Phillip Banks.

He was even better looking now. And, oh, my, he was hot.

Nerves danced in her stomach. Frankie bounced in her beribboned heels, wondering if this was what Cinderella had felt like when she'd spotted the prince at the ball.

Half delighted, half terrified.

And totally turned on.

**Pick up CHRISTMAS WITH A SEAL
by Tawny Weber in November 2014
wherever you buy Harlequin® Blaze® books!**

Copyright © 2014 by Tawny Weber

HBEXP79823

Holiday nights are heating up!

Lucy Vandenburg decides to end her dating dry spell in one naughty, uninhibited night with a sexy stranger. But the man she chooses turns out to be someone she knows all too well....

Don't miss

Oh, Naughty Night!

from *New York Times* bestselling author

Leslie Kelly

Available November 2014
wherever you buy Harlequin Blaze books.

HARLEQUIN®

Blaze®

Red-Hot Reads
www.Harlequin.com

HB79824

Thrill Seeker!

Adventure guide Ryan Quinn's job was easy: escort übercelebrity Serena Hightower and her bridesmaids around Fiji. But when he and Serena discover a sizzling chemistry, they'll risk everything for the most thrilling adventure yet!

From the reader-favorite
The Mighty Quinns miniseries,

The Mighty Quinns: Ryan
by *Kate Hoffman*

Available November 2014
wherever you buy Harlequin Blaze books.

H HARLEQUIN®

Blaze®
Red-Hot Reads
www.Harlequin.com

HB79825

JUST CAN'T GET ENOUGH?

Join our social communities
and talk to us online.

You will have access to the latest
news on upcoming titles and special
promotions, but most importantly,
you can talk to other fans about your
favorite Harlequin reads.

Harlequin.com/Community

Facebook.com/HarlequinBooks

Twitter.com/HarlequinBooks

Pinterest.com/HarlequinBooks

HSOCIAL